DARK HORIZON

A NOVEL

MICHAEL DAVID

THE PEARL OF SPIRITUALITY SHINES BRIGHTEST
AMIDST THE HEART OF DARKNESS.

DARK HORIZON

SOLASTA
PRESS

an imprint of
OGHMA CREATIVE MEDIA

OGHMA

C R E A T I V E   M E D I A

Solasta Press
An imprint of Oghma Creative Media, Inc.
2401 Beth Lane, Bentonville, Arkansas 72712

Library of Congress Cataloging-in-Publication Data

Names: David, Michael, author.
Title: Dark Horizon/Michael David. |
Description: First Edition. | Bentonville: Solasta, 2019.
Identifiers: LCCN: 2018955936 | ISBN: 978-1-63373-459-3 (hardcover) |
ISBN: 978-1-63373-460-9 (trade paperback) | ISBN: 978-1-63373-461-6 (eBook)
Subjects: | BISAC: FICTION/Thrillers/Supernatural |
FICTION/Thrillers/Psychological | FICTION/Thrillers/Suspense
LC record available at: https://lccn.loc.gov/2018955936

Solasta Press trade paperback edition April, 2019

Cover & Interior Design by Casey W. Cowan
Editing by Gil Miller & George "Clay" Mitchell

For Dewanna Pace.
Your memory lives on.

I am deeply grateful to my wife, Janet, and her support of my writing.

PROLOGUE

THE TWILIGHT
OF ATLANTIS

THE TROPICAL BREEZE DRIFTED ACROSS the uppermost bay of Northern Atlantis, offering the metropolis solace from the evening heat. As it crept inland to the center of the city, it caressed the edge of the Temple's parted curtains and shifted the diaphanous material before it died on the hem of Amelius's purple robe.

The leader of Northern Atlantis struggled with his emotions while the rays from the setting sun moved closer to the crown of a three-foot crystal in the center of the priest's chamber. He felt the jackhammer of his heart beating against his chest. Momentarily, the room's only door silently opened. He wiped at the sweat upon his brow and looked at the shrouded, white-robed oracle when she stepped into the room. Her eyes sparkled and crinkled in the corners when she smiled at him. The seer wobbled slightly, creating a distinctive click with her right foot while her left brushed softly against stone.

Amelius's granddaughter knelt in front of the crystal and clasped her hands, bowing her head just as the evening sun impacted the crystal's apex. The glow birthed an ambient yellow that rose through the shaft before expanding outward to bathe the room in a soft spiritual radiance. An etching on the side of the crystal threw an image of a human eye centered inside a pyramid upon the wall.

Amelius took a deep breath and stood transfixed by the light, barely noticing that his dusky red skin now appeared bronze.

In a moment of self-condemnation, Amelius knew he'd waited too long. How many innocent people would die because of his inaction? A muscle twitched in his eyelid. Bitter fear always remained at the edge of his thoughts. Should he have petitioned the Prophet's Crystal sooner?

In the past year, he'd struggled to forge a diplomatic solution to what was inarguably the greatest conflict between Atlantis's ethical north and the selfish south. The dilemma involved the enslavement of genetically engineered sub-humans, or "automatons," as a captive workforce by the industrial and agricultural sectors. Tensions had simmered between the divided factions of the island nation and finally culminated two days ago with a demand from the north to end the enslavement of the "workforce." The south's response was ruthless. "You have two days. Accept them as slaves or face total destruction."

With the deadline less than two hours away, Amelius turned to the Prophet's Crystal. When the evening sun shone fully upon the mineral's crown, a connection with the Divine Being was forged.

Amelius knew that to question the God of One, a human conduit of humble purity was required. It also demanded an even greater rarity—one whose heart and soul were above reproach.

A century ago, Amelius had been that conduit. He'd forged connections through the Prophet's Crystal many times, but decades of political intrigue had weakened his morality, denying him unconditional purity. Now, there was only one seer who had the heart to ask the question that plagued Amelius and his people.

The young oracle, Aiyala, lifted her head and spread her arms to embrace the light. She inhaled deeply of the golden essence within the room, causing it to ripple and pulse as it slowly began to revolve around her.

Pain stabbed through Amelius's temple because he feared the connection would fail, that somehow Aiyala would be found lacking. Each second brought gruesome thoughts that attacked his waning confidence. He stared at the shrouded oracle, willing her to connect, praying that she had not fallen from grace like he had.

The light in the chamber pulsed to the beat of a human heart, and all sounds from within the Temple ceased. The air throbbed with static charge and Amelius's senses heightened. He re-experienced a sacred quickening which birthed a familiar feeling—the overwhelming presence of supreme divinity. He could never put into words the deep peace and inherent love that came from connecting with the God of One.

Yet, Amelius knew from the past that he was experiencing a fraction of what Aiyala felt. Sadness filled his heart for having lost his way, thus diluting the full effect of Divine connection.

Centered within her luminous aura--she stood confidently—much in the vein of someone more mature. "Show the path, oh God of One, so that we may free the enslaved." Her voice resonated with internal strength.

Within moments, a three-dimensional figure of Atlantis materialized above the crystal in the amber mist. The majestic buildings and homes of the northern metropolis gleamed within the Divine projection, while the verdant fields and massive factories of the south sprawled into view.

From the working faction of his former spiritual self, Amelius intuited the darkness that would fall upon his land. He knew the fate of his people. Ten million citizens doomed.

The Divine image confirmed his greatest fear by showing the treachery of the south. Their armada of lighter-than-air crafts were deploying this very moment, in a preemptive strike against the north. The fleet was armed with the devastating power of their offensive crystals.

Even though the crafts were just taking off, the image revealed what would happen when they arrived. Massive shafts of energy pulsed from their war machines and impacted the earth. Violent explosions followed, giving rise to the screams of the injured and the dying.

Amelius felt bile rise to his throat. Cities were leveled. Towering fire consumed the dead and those too maimed to flee.

No one would survive.

The image faded and the ambient light around Aiyala dissipated. She struggled upright and dropped her shroud. When she looked up, Amelius recoiled from the fear in her eyes.

She cried out, "Grandfather!"

He rushed to Aiyala and embraced her. The power of total love commanded him to protect her, and with that he formed a desperate plan. Amelius brushed away the auburn hair on her forehead. "You must leave now. Take the Prophet's Crystal and our last weapon—before our cities are destroyed."

Aiyala cried in anguish and Amelius brushed the tears streaming down her face. He looked deep within her pleading eyes. "My place is here with my people and I choose to die with them as long as I know you're safe."

Aiyala moved to retrieve the crystal, causing her right foot to click and slide upon the stone floor once again.

Amelius glanced at her "foot"—a cloven hoof—connected to a misshapen goat's leg that finally melded into human flesh.

She met Amelius's eyes, and said, "I know our surgeons could have corrected this. Yet, it is my mark."

Amelius knew the story well. Eons ago, before there were humans on Earth, the present citizens of Atlantis were spiritual thought forms with a desire to experience physical reality. Eager to encounter life, they pushed into materiality, using the earth's animals and God's image for mankind as a pattern. The results were a blend of human and animal features that eventually evolved into the true Sons and Daughters of God.

Amelius wiped at his tears.

Aiyala pleaded with her eyes. "Even though I am a far descendent from the original thought forms, my deformity has always been a blessing because it reminds me of my origin." She tried to smile. "You've always said that life is a circle and you and I shall be together throughout time."

The thought of never seeing his granddaughter in this life terrified him more than his imminent death.

Aiyala straightened her body as much as her leg allowed. "The Prophet's Crystal imparted a final vision. I will journey by air machine to a faraway land, one which will later be called Texas. It is there that I will bury the two crystals. I will live through many reincarnations, but in twelve-thousand years my destiny will be to face the leader of the south and exact retribution for the destruction of Atlantis."

Amelius and Aiyala hugged each other, neither wanting to leave. But when the heavy thump of far-off explosions broke the silence, it also shattered what remained of Amelius's heart. He rose to his full height, towering over Aiyala, the cords in his neck strained. "Those bringing destruction to Atlantis will face karmic justice. Now go, Aiyala. Go, before it's too late."

DARK HORIZON

AVE
MARIA

IN THE GLOW OF A single light, a completely nude Morda took his garden shears and snipped his prisoner's little finger off.

Bound to a metal chair, the man rammed his torso against the back of the chair, shrieking. "I told you the truth! I took the money. It's all in that letter."

Morda placed the piece of paper on a small table. "I know you told the truth. But what I'm doing now has nothing to do with stealing from the syndicate. You see, I'm in the mood for some fun. And that creates another benefit. When your body is found, its condition will deliver a message to your fellow conspirators."

He positioned the next three fingers on the table, which soaked the incriminating letter until it was bright red. But he wasn't through. For the next hour, he kept his prey alive and aware. The growing pile of body parts spread his victim's blood across the table and onto the floor below.

Finally, Morda drew a scalpel across the man's neck, leaving a gushing red incision in its wake. Arterial blood shot across the room in a powerful arc. With each waning heartbeat, it pulsed lower until it gradually subsided. A weak dribble signaled death. Morda wiped the blade on the dead man's shirt.

Another loose end tied up. Another contract finished. Another sum of money in the bank.

Yet another diversion from the monotony of island life.

Morda turned the light off and padded across the floor to lie upon his expansive bed. His hairless body was firm with feminine curves. When he shifted slightly, erotic friction between satin sheets and smooth flesh caused him to sigh. Beside him was a man's wig of brown human hair, resting upon a European goose-down pillow. He set it on his smooth head and licked the tip of his forefinger, greedily sucking its tartness and salt. Morda closed his eyes and traced the wet tip across his stomach, traveling lower until he whimpered from the intimate touch. Once there, he encountered what made him uniquely Morda. A textbook hermaphrodite, he had both a pussy and a dick. Today, he identified as a male, while tomorrow he might choose to be female.

Moving from the shadows to play at the foot of his bed, Janette, the blind German violinist, stated her presence with an unholy rendition of *Ave Maria*. A pale shaft of moonlight stirred the shadows while her tainted music filled the room. Through consummate genius, she crafted her rendition to twist and break the spirit of an uplifting song.

Her savage bow and forceful fingers seemed to rape the Stradivarius, making it scream with outrage, giving life to sounds of soiled spirituality.

Twisted strains of a once holy song died harshly in the night, and Morda stirred with purpose. Supple as a cat, he rose and strode to the base of the bed to stare into Janette's sightless eyes. He enjoyed the bright pink flush of her cheeks, her pursed lips and the crisp white linen of her blouse that emphasized hardened nipples. Her body heat radiated outward, and for a moment he reflected. With rare praise, he acknowledged the performance. "Stunning."

Each encounter that mocked the grace and laws of God drew Morda closer to his inner darkness. Struggling to reach what he feared most, he begged for that which would destroy him.

Balling his fists on his rounded hips, he stuck his lower lip out in a pout. "You know the way out, Janette. It's time for you to leave."

He strode to the window and gazed upon the fluid darkness of the Mediterranean. Far below, luminescent surf crashed against the base of the cliff, sending its spray upwards. The essence of saltwater embraced his bare skin with its moist touch, seeping into his pores and exploring each crevice of his body.

He cocked his head and heard the shuffle of his elderly caretaker.

Antonio appeared and averted his eyes from the dead man. "You have a phone call, *Signore.*"

He drew a long, slow breath, and smiled while the servant's wrinkled hand shook around the outstretched smartphone.

Morda glanced at the wall clock and his heart jerked into a rapid, adrenalized beat. He'd expected this call. "Hello?"

Static crackled in the background and a polite, elderly man answered, *"The project at the Sphinx is progressing. Just as the Christian Prophet foretold, a man of singular faith will discover the tunnel tomorrow night, beneath the right paw. The authorities have been persuaded to… not interfere, so it's imperative you leave for Cairo soon. You are our insurance on the team's performance."* A thin laugh erupted. *"Payment, of course, will be through usual channels, half now and half when you're done. As long as you retrieve the Atlantean crystal my employer desires."*

The line went dead and Morda handed the phone back to the caretaker.

Seconds slipped by and the Mediterranean murmured below. Antonio swallowed and kept his eyes averted. "Will that be all?"

Morda turned in dismissal. "Get rid of the body."

Antonio clenched his teeth, glanced at Morda's back, and crossed himself. In a voice heavy with fear, he whispered, "Our Father who art in Heaven…."

DARK SECRETS
WITHIN

RISING ABOVE THE TEXAS PLAINS, blustery skies whipped fallow earth into a towering wall of ephemeral darkness. With stoic acceptance, the sun-baked vista called Amarillo claimed a brief respite before its presence dimmed to shadows.

Within the city's domain, a merciless summer had waned to a sullen fall. Strangled weeds whipped against decaying fences. Buildings creaked from dust-laden wind. Awnings shook, and trash raced along deserted streets. In the choked sunlight, tattered homes stretched outward while a faded sign proclaimed, *Mother Sonja—Palm Reader.*

Spreading within the once prosperous home, darkness suckled itself and copulated with the smell of decay. There, in the house's small foyer, a dusty Bible lay open, marked by the drippings of guttering candles. Curled at the edges, Jesus's picture hung above, thumb-tacked to a peeling wall.

In the foyer's semi-darkness, Mother Sonja tapped her size three flip-flop against the cracked linoleum. The mantel clock hiccupped in constipated whirs, expelling four explosive chimes. The fifth arrived seconds later.

Down the hallway, a faint rustle preceded the heavy scratch of claws upon worn carpet. Churchill, the one-eyed bulldog, sauntered with confidence to the edge of the linoleum, ignoring Mother Sonja with studied indifference. A black patch held in place by a thin elastic band barely covered his left eye.

"Little one…." She stared through milky eyes, unable to distinguish the shape on her left.

The clock gave another half-hearted whir while the wind rattled the front door. Outside, a car door slammed and Churchill snorted. He gave Mother Sonja a doggy grin, lifted his hind leg and dribbled unceremoniously upon the foyer wall. With an air of mastery, he turned and strutted back to the kitchen.

She squinted at the vague, receding shape. "You're such a good boy." A knock announced her next customer and the psychic turned to open the door, only to be overwhelmed by hot, dry, wind that licked hungrily at her wrinkled brown toes. She looked in the direction of her client and birthed a smile that was deceptively warm. A false front of warmth encouraged trust with those coming for psychic readings. As a result, they disclosed information they would never share under normal circumstances.

From an early age, Mother Sonja's psychic ability had been recognized and encouraged by her Romani grandmother, who devoted daily sessions to palm reading and the finer aspects of separating the client from his money. The prodigy child surpassed all her mentor's expectations by giving the customers the answers to their questions. Names, dates, and places were always given, and later proved to be true.

Mother Sonja's eyes darted from side to side as she shoved the screen door open. The wind slammed it against the house, covering her soft greeting, "Come in, come in."

SHERRY STEPPED INSIDE THE FOYER and brushed her mass of tangled hair into place. With a quick look around, she focused on her reflection in the mirror. At thirty-seven, she was fortunate to have a slender build, despite the effects of her medication. She'd inherited her father's dark brown hair and wore it long and curly, with only a trace of silver. Friends said her green eyes and petite, upturned nose were appealing, yet an inner vibrancy shone through, and from that emerged her true beauty.

With a quick turn, she appraised the psychic before her. Mother Sonja stood five feet tall and her skin was wrinkled and darkened from the harsh Texas sun. Her face portrayed the striking angles of Native Americans, while her colorful, ethnic clothes reflected the depth and passion of Romani heritage. Time and character had imprinted upon the psychic's face, leaving a message which spoke to Sherry.

She cocked her head, and listened to a still, small voice within. Weigh the words spoken through this channel and sift the chaff from the grain.

Sherry bit her lower lip. She possessed the ability to gain insight, yet this inner thought hammered against the reality of living with schizophrenia, leaving her in torment over the validity of its message. She wondered if this small voice was a true perception or the twisted rape of genetic illness? Momentarily shaken, she looked at the floor in shame.

Mother Sonja touched Sherry's bare arm, sliding worn fingers down and across her charm bracelet. The psychic's wizened face warmed. "You come with questions?"

Reassured from the woman's touch, Sherry looked up. "I do."

"Call me Mother Sonja."

"I'm Sherry. I want to…."

The tiny psychic spread her arms and spawned an indulgent smile. "Someone you love is almost on other side." She nodded sagely and arched an eyebrow. "Mother Sonja has power to keep him alive."

Without another word, Sherry turned and followed her into the shadowy living room. A joyless shaft of caramel light struggled through aging tapestries and stirred the sullen hush of darkness. An overture of autumn shadows grudgingly revealed a torn couch of somber complexion.

The two sat and the meager sunlight divided them. On one side, the light amplified Mother Sonja's harsh features. On the opposite, it embellished Sherry's softness and youth. The psychic gently took Sherry's right hand, brushed it open, and ran her palm a finger's breadth over her client's.

The psychic pondered for a moment. "Mother Sonja sees many things."

Intrigued, Sherry bent forward.

"You come across like a woman of simple ways. You want to appear, what would some say, ordinary?" The psychic narrowed her eyes. "Your inner mind is a house of many rooms, each one uncommon and different from the norm. Most people don't understand what lies beneath your facade, because you allow few into your home."

Mother Sonja tapped her gnarled finger against Sherry's palm, and the silence in the room defined the moment with a presence of its own. The psychic closed her eyes. "I am with you, Sherry, and see inside your hidden room. Within this chamber of twisted shadows and dark reflections is a shrouded mirror. When I part its folds, I see your sister of shame. Schizophrenia. You hide her name, for to think it, brings her to life.

"Her face is twisted and ugly and Satan delights in her work. When the devil's maid looks upon you, she drags your soul into horrible, horrible hell." Mother Sonja's brow wrinkled. "When this demon touches you, morning's light finds your mind stuck in the slime of immobility, and evening's twilight spawns a thousand thoughts with no direction or end. When you are consumed by this disease, there is no balance of reality, for light bows to the power of darkness."

A knot formed in Sherry's throat and she tried to swallow.

"But when your mental illness subsides, the tainted demon gives you her most horrible gift. She leaves you with memory of your actions, and you are impaled with shame." Mother Sonja breathed deeply. "People do not understand your schizophrenia, and you shy from your peers. How can friendships thrive on the edge of damnation? Yet, after these living hells, there is one who knew and understood." Mother Sonja said simply, "I hear his voice, clearly. He cares."

Sherry took a quick breath.

"This one you have come to learn about... Grandfather." Tension twisted Mother Sonja's voice and perspiration dotted her forehead. "I see him soon in gathering. The realm of departed souls." She whispered, "Grandfather is dying."

Sherry steadied herself on the couch, catching her heart-shaped charm on a rip.

"He will pass to the plane of newly dead." The psychic jerked her head toward some unseen presence. Her eyes glazed, and her face twisted into harsh angles. "Sherry, you must help me." A masculine plea, in Grandfather's voice, wrenched from her throat. "You have to listen to her. Mother Sonja can help."

Sherry's eyes opened wide.

The psychic raised her head and begged again in Grandfather's voice, "Do whatever she asks."

At that moment, Sherry was aware of a strange vibration coming from Mother Sonja's palm onto the tips of her fingers. Without knowing why, she clasped the psychic's hand firmly.

Mother Sonja took a deep breath and shuddered. Her teeth clicked. Her eyelids fluttered just as the trance ended. The psychic pleaded, "You must believe me. Your Grandfather is going to pass. I can keep him from dying."

Still unsure, Sherry nodded.

Mother Sonja moved closer. "I pray for your grandfather, because I have special power. But..." She let the words die a troubled death and smiled. "It takes time. And money."

Sherry still held on to the psychic's palm, and the vibration grew stronger. She averted her gaze and shifted her eyes upward and to the left. It was then the power of spirit expanded her inner world. Mother Sonja still talked, but the words were slow and muffled, like echoes down a distant tunnel.

Sherry was aware of being in two places at once. In one sense, she was sitting on the couch with Mother Sonja, yet there was more. The alternate panorama communicated in deep spiritual absolutes, never being shadowed by doubt's presence. A peculiar feeling stated that she'd never left this world, that somehow, she'd been asleep all of her life and was now awake.

The vision spoke in pieces and fragments, until the incongruency gave way to a feeling of spiritual eloquence. Grandfather was bathed in pastel hues, and stood before Sherry as a healthy man, proudly erect and free of illness.

In the soft, vibrant light, he smiled. "Fear not, Sherry. My time is near and I have made my decision. I will not die until you're here with me." The love of a lifetime spoke in the words of the heart, and the presence of peace dwelt within her.

The vision lived within the deeper sense of truth and comfort filled the space of the spirit's realm. That calmness dispelled all fear, and she accepted her mentor's words.

Grandfather delivered a cryptic message. "Beneath the dead zone, Sherry. Find the cause and you will find your way."

Sherry let go of Mother Sonja's palm and the image faded to shades of gray. Even though the voice the psychic had channeled sounded like Grandfather's, there was no doubt about his true message. She shifted her eyes and travelled back to reality.

With confidence born of practice, Mother Sonja delivered her solution. "For three hundred dollars, I pray to angels. They keep your Grandfather from passing."

The rage was slow to ignite. Using an ability she didn't quite understand, Sherry psychically tuned in to this woman and saw her history of deception and betrayal. Fifty years of milking her clients for money with false readings was condensed in a rush of images. Mother Sonja's duplicity enraged Sherry, and she trembled with anger. "Long ago you were given a precious gift by God, bestowed in the spirit of grace. Yet you used your psychic ability for the sake of ego." Sherry took a shaky breath. "In your twisted mind, you also did it for the satisfaction of personal gain. Because you could."

Mother Sonja looked up. Disbelief etched her face.

"There have been countless people who've come to you for guidance. Not only have you taken their money, you've gloated over their pain. You never intended to help. You're the worst kind of thief, for you steal from God." Sherry jerked her arm back, and the charm ripped from her bracelet. "You are the vilest form of trash, and I'll expose you for what you are."

Something dark and ugly twisted Mother Sonja's face into a malevolent mask. With unnatural strength, she slapped Sherry hard.

The violent impact twisted her head.

Sherry stood. Her legs nearly buckled. Her face burned with indignation, yet truth and justness were her companions. With all the dignity she could muster, she turned to leave, no longer a partner to Mother Sonja's scheme.

THE DOOR SLAMMED, AND SILENCE became the uneasy bedfellow to Mother Sonja's harsh breathing. Wind buffeted the window above her and the sound of Sherry's car roared into the distance. Minutes passed while flecks of foam dribbled over her lips and down her chin. But the pensive hush aborted when Churchill snorted. Strutting his way to the edge of the room, the bulldog cocked his head and stared defiantly at its master.

Mother Sonja took a ragged breath and in a honeyed voice enticed her true master, "Come to me, Darkness. Oh… unholy lover." Her eyes jerked in violent unison and she twisted spasmodically. Leaning on the couch's arm, her body stiffened. A thin stream of urine stained her clothing and ran down her leg.

Churchill snorted indifferently.

The tiny psychic lay in her urine and trembled, and as the light faded, the clock chimed the half-hour. At that moment, something moved amid the smell of piss and decay. A shadow, darker than the rest, drifted from the bowels of darkness and pulsed heavily. Its unholy presence gave birth to an unnatural cold.

Churchill blinked his good eye and exhaled a tiny puff of frosty air.

Mother Sonja jerked again, aware of her soiled clothes and the puddle at her feet. The epicenter of coldness centered itself around her, and fresh foam bubbled between her lips. She gagged and blinked her eyes—eyes that felt on fire and burned with the fury of hell's Sabbath. A vague glint upon the couch caught her attention and she groped with gnarled fingers until she lifted Sherry's cold, heart-shaped charm.

She closed her hand, pressing the charm into her palm. Opening her mind to Sherry's energy, images rushed forward.

Over twelve thousand years ago, Mother Sonja was the leader of southern Atlantis and had turned the offensive power of her lighter-than-air warships upon the opposing force of northern Atlantis. Amid the sounds of devastating energy bolts, the ground air sizzled with carnage and screams of the dying.

But, the wily Amelius had foreseen the attack and helped his granddaughter, Aiyala, escape with the Prophet's Crystal and one offensive weapon.

She immediately saw her age-old nemesis, Aiyala, as the present-day incarnation of Sherry. The psychic also knew that karma would soon be served or subverted and that one of them might be dead before this was over.

Holding Sherry's charm up to the light, her face twisted in sweet anticipation. With the conviction of Satan's spawn, the psychic swore. "You don't fuck with Mother Sonja."

THE AWAKENING

DEATH HUNG HEAVY IN THE AIR, fetid, peculiarly uncomfortable. Sherry passed by rooms of the dying. The smell of excrement and urine, she understood, even accepted. But the other, that scent of inescapable death, tightened the back of her throat, leaving a ball of saliva. She would never be ready to accept this predator.

Pastel walls reflected the distant morning light and a radio played some forgotten tune. Somewhere, a phone rang twelve times and stopped.

Here, in death's midst, Sherry entered her grandfather's room and the faded quality of autumn sunlight extended itself to the foot of his bed. Kind and noble, this patient man waited. Subtly present, grandfather's dignity spoke to those who would hear. When he felt stronger, they would laugh, share some insight. Then they'd pray.

Some were in hospice before their journey started, most others at its end. This patient gentleman waited for profound transition.

Sherry stood beside him and he slowly opened his eyes. His pupils were glossy, opaque, but an inner vibrancy sparked, moments before the smile touched his face. Lifting his gnarled hand to wave left him tired.

Sherry's heart ached as she circled his hand with hers. Squeezing lightly, she willed her warmth to his cold.

"How are you, Sherry?"

His words were somehow comforting, and they supported her illusion that he would live. "Fine," she replied. Nothing more.

Grandfather's eyes spoke of caring. "The hallucination?"

With those two words, Sherry's shame flared. Schizophrenia. A profound demon. Her tormentor. Since she was twelve, the illness had hounded her. She was thirty-seven now. But this gentleman understood, and he cared.

"It's better." She brushed back his thinning white hair. "I've a new medicine." When she ended her thought, a whisper of fabric rustled from behind. She turned to see two oil field workers at the door. Her response was quick and heartfelt, "Lightfeather."

The weathered Comanche Indian stepped softly, his long white hair framing a strong face. Beside him was someone new, a man with broad shoulders and quiet strength.

"I'm Cadence McShane." The man's words were flavored with a slow West Texan drawl.

His calloused handshake was firm and his brown eyes evaluated Sherry.

With a glance at the Indian, he crossed his arms. "Lightfeather speaks well of you."

Her attention faltered. Without warning, the images bombarded her. At the mercy of her illness, it was like she was watching a scene from her past. There was no correlation to reality as visual bits and pieces cascaded her consciousness. With it, discord blossomed—a short-circuiting of the brain ensued. That bastard intrusion raped Sherry's mind, overwhelmed her resistance, and left her skewed and vulnerable.

The hallucination played before her mind's eye. It was the same, and always in black and white. A deserted field was covered with hundreds of pumpkins, stacked one upon the other, rising over six feet high. At the bottom of the pile lay a straw scarecrow, dressed in shabby pants and a chambray shirt. A large butcher knife glistened with blood and slashed downward, again and again, eviscerating the scarecrow, leaving straw and shredded cloth to scatter in the fickle wind.

In the space of a microsecond, Sherry had become intimate with madness. "Who will save the Scarecrow Man?" she answered Cadence from the realm of mental darkness.

Cadence glanced at Lightfeather. She read his confusion and was a victim to its aftermath.

Most laymen thought schizophrenics weren't aware of their actions. She begged to differ. She was painfully aware of everything. There was not the blessed forgetfulness of irrational behaviors. Even though it was a chemical imbalance, she was extremely vulnerable. Just now, while she spoke out of context, she felt Cadence's confusion. And, truly, Sherry suffered from it. She was caught between heaven and hell, forever tugged between the two yet belonging to neither.

Years before, Sherry wasn't conscious of the short-circuiting. There was no recognition of the process. She was subject to the random act of neurotransmitters and remained blissfully ignorant. But when she finally got the right meds, she was aware of her insanity. It was ironic when you knew you were crazy. It chafed her to think of the next medical breakthrough.

Compounding the situation further, her incredible sensitivity registered people's reactions. The subtle aversion of their eyes, that doubtful stare. She was destroyed most effectively with the undisguised fear she saw on faces.

Media-induced images were swallowed by a gullible public who stereotyped all schizophrenics as dangerous and psychotic. The majority of them were harmless, trapped in a damning reality beyond their control. The sane might have understood the illness in some detached manner, but they would never truly know what it felt like.

Unless they breached the edge of darkness. Those that did rarely came back. But, Sherry was caught in between the light and the dark.

With her new sensitivity, she had learned a cruel and unusual lesson. Cover up her shame or be branded, marked by her guilt. Apologizing for actions over which she had no control didn't mix well with her self-esteem. But then, life was often unfair. With a practiced air of assurance, she addressed Cadence, "Sometimes my thoughts come with a life of their own." Her smile hid the discomfort.

Cadence turned his brown eyes upon her and smiled back. "I know."

Embarrassment cascaded through Sherry's mind—the chagrin of acknowledgment, that knowing of her illness, filled her with dread. She retreated quietly, to sit in a worn, brown recliner and let her emotions settle. The two men turned toward Grandfather, and she contrasted their features.

Lightfeather stood the taller of the two, older and dignified, and lent a spiritual authority to the room. His face was strong, gracefully sculpted with timeless honor. Perhaps it was won through patience and acceptance. Sherry thought he wore his lessons well.

While Lightfeather talked to his dying friend, she focused on Cadence. Always uncomfortable with her uncanny ability to read people, he was a dichotomy of spirituality and something dark. Most people wouldn't pick up on it, for the undercurrent of violence was overlaid by his gentleness. If you knew how to look, a face would tell you its story. As she stared, his attentive eyes shifted to hers, acknowledging her interest.

For a middle-aged man, probably thirty-nine or forty, he was in remarkable shape. Lean and powerful with shimmering, obsidian hair, Cadence presented an easy-going persona. His slow West Texan drawl fanned her interest and his eyes reflected sexual attraction.

His gaze shifted, and she couldn't help but wonder what he thought of her. She had been told inner vibrancy was her true beauty, but she liked to think her intelligence was an asset, too. When she was on medication and stabilized, she had a keen interest in the working of the human mind. Sherry had started college as a Psychology major, but switched to a Med-Evac Technician so she could join the local search and rescue helicopter. Not knowing how or why, she had an uncanny ability to help find lost people.

Even though her grip on reality was rarely taken for granted, one of several uncomfortable gifts had always remained—the ability to read people's underlying motivations. At times, it was unnerving. From a glance, she could tell whether someone was good or evil, and subsequent events would bear her out.

As the two turned to leave, Sherry acknowledged her attraction to Cadence. If the message in his eyes spoke true, there was interest on his part as well. She shifted in the brown recliner and leaned back. Her smile signaled heartfelt thanks to the two men and she couldn't help but think of the pleasure they had brought Grandfather.

A strong remnant of crude oil remained in the room and the faded sunlight warmed her cheek. She was lulled into calm reverie until Grandfather's voice startled her with its urgency.

"Sherry?"

She moved to his side. "Yes?" Her heart ached, for his eyes were dull. He raised his hand and it shook badly.

"You must forgive Sabra."

Sherry flinched. "I've tried."

"In her way, your mother loves you. Don't forget."

She caressed his warm hand. Now, hers was cold. "Ever since my… schizophrenia, she's someone else." Sherry closed her eyes. "We're the Whittingtons. Insanity doesn't happen to the rich and privileged. I'm an outcast. I'm mentally ill. Does she speak about me to her high society friends? Her precious daughter?"

"In time, she will.…"

He coughed violently, twisted his frail body.

"… understand."

Her friend and confidant, her mentor, was too weak to move. He lay spent upon a large pillow, his parched skin unnaturally pale.

"Grandfather?" Sherry's words were empty, but her heart asked for a miracle. "I'm… fine."

His statement was as cold as her hope. With a will that had long since died, she slowly stepped away. The brown recliner patiently waited to embrace her worried body. She dropped into the worn cushions, only to send dust motes into the fading sunlight.

Her soul was overloaded with grief and something broke within. Her mind gently knocked—to open that secret door.

Sherry entered this private realm to be free of anguish. Blessedly, she was embraced by calming peace. She looked around the hospice room and her senses were acute. A lone dust speck rose high above the rest. With her finger, she touched it, only to stir its companions into the light.

The air was dry, and her lips were chapped. In the space of moments, she had shed emotional assault to embrace comfort. Gratefully, the calming presence filled her senses with the elixir of inner peace. And graciously, she took her fill.

This was the plane of angels. Here, they showered comfort upon her troubled soul. In her secret room, the spiritual essence was like sacred space. It was an encompassing reassurance that rewarded unshakable faith. In spite of her fear of death, she passionately believed in something beyond its finality.

Some might think this the Band-Aid of the mentally ill, but that part of her, her faith, was untainted and free of illness. With unshakable innocence, she believed.

From this vista, she was separated from the negative emotions of his dying. Sherry looked upon Grandfather without the feelings of guilt, anger, or remorse. In its place, she was an observer from a profound point. The emotional comfort was positive, and its power grew. She was filled with the knowledge of this transitional event. Death was not negative or fearful. For strange as it seemed, she was overwhelmed with the rightness of holy transition.

"Sherry?"

She pulled away from her thoughts, yet the comfort persisted.

"We own major oil." He coughed, twisting his body again. "Your mother. More money than sense. Cut from her will...."

His eyes began to lose focus.

"Damn her. You deserve. Last wish... my will."

She moved to his side, and gently placed her hand against his cheek. "Money's not important." His face was dangerously white, yet he curled the edge of his lips and tried to smile.

"Where nothing grows. Beneath the dead zone, Sherry."

Slowly and with knowing, he rolled his head away. His speckled skin stretched tautly over pronounced bones, and he sighed deeply.

"I love you so much," Sherry spoke with the gentleness of a child.

Grandfather's erratic breathing reverberated in the silence that consumed them. For within this last communion, she was awash with the sacredness of the moment. Most people have never experienced what she felt, for when we left the physical and entered the spiritual, there could be no fear. It cannot exist in a realm of total love. Spirituality encompassed her, and she peacefully accepted it. It was a warmth in her soul. If she could have seen what she felt, it would have been a white light amidst a host of angels.

On Earth, we are bound by our senses. If you hear something, it's real. You don't deny it. The same for sight, smell, touch, and taste. In the physical world, we experience through the senses yet receive only a fraction of that which is possible. Knowing so little, we think we walk on true ground. But in God's realm, there is communication on many levels. You have to feel the presence, experience the understanding. Only then will you know much deeper truths.

The warm wholeness of total love warmed her soul and she understood. Grandfather's hand grew cold, and the secret chamber opened once more.

In her vision, Sherry was no longer in the hospice room, for she stood at the bottom of a stairwell. Light clearly showed the path. Seven steps of pine, freshly sanded, awaited her while she savored the smell of new varnish.

Something urged her, so she climbed. Sherry's hand glided along the burnished wooden banister, and she focused directly ahead. Gently, she opened the door to enter a small, dark room. The smell of burning oak filled the space, for a fire blazed in the back and flickered across a dark, polished desk. Behind the wooden furniture stood a short, black-robed monk who waited patiently as Sherry evaluated him. His hair was neatly shaved from his head, and he stood ready to speak.

Yet something made her uneasy, for his eyes spoke of the Apollonian way. They sparkled in the firelight with truth and the way of God. But deeper within, lay tainted darkness. In his hands rested an open, weathered book, black, with gilt-edged pages. A cryptic smile gave his eyes a sensual flicker.

"I am Pablo. Guide of good and evil."

He shifted the book slightly, signaling his source of power. Pablo stood with assurance, commanded the room with his presence.

"Within these pages, my child, lies the way of human nature."

He stroked the dark lettered page, gently, almost fearfully.

"You were put upon this earth for a purpose. When you were young and pure, you faced your path. Before you laid good and evil, life and death, and you chose."

Pablo's unnerving gaze coupled with hers. His voice resonated over the crackling fire.

"You chose wisely."

Sherry broke eye contact and stared at the floor, for the cloying edge of fear rose in her chest.

"But on that fateful day, you lost your way. You became disillusioned in the world around you. In defense of your weakness, you offered explanations. 'It wasn't my fault. It was forced on me.' And so, you chose to believe."

The priest of the Apollonian way spoke calmly to her illusion.

"As you say, Sherry, then shall you believe. Your refusal to accept your true self poisoned your outlook. From this vista, you chose unwisely. Your thoughts turned angry—negative and self-destructive. Now your mind is confused, beset with trouble. But, with each trial, God prepares an escape."

She stared at the flickering fire within his eyes.

"You may still right the path and find your way."

Turning a gilt-edged page, Pablo tapped a thick finger upon the text.

"The information given sets before you personal expectations. In the ensuing days, you will embark on a journey and choose a path that will advance your soul or bring spiritual defeat."

Pablo's red tongue slid across his lips. "First, you must accept the Spirit of the Awakening. This will not be easy, but once it is completed, more knowledge will come. In your journey, you have started the sacred path. Advancement depends upon you."

Pablo sighed and closed the book. For a heartbeat Sherry reflected, and the moment faded within her secret room. Closing her mind to an alternate reality, the image within swirled softly in vibrant hues, with teasing pastels amid blue borders.

She blinked and Grandfather's cold hand slowly came back into her frame of focus. Endowed with the understanding of mystics, Sherry basked in the glow of divine presence. The rightness of his sacred transition empowered her with total acceptance.

Yet, as she reflected, a lifetime of warnings from Mother and Father against psychic experiences coated her consciousness with the thick paste of fear. Sherry struggled to make sense of this vision of holiness.

Was it really good?

Or, like her parents had warned, was it true evil?

LIFE IS BUT A
DREAM

HIDDEN FROM THE FUNERAL, SHERRY watched a sprinkler casting water in a graceful arc, creating a living rainbow that shimmered on the edge of morning light. Brilliant colors sparkled across cool air and cascaded to the grass below. Within these forty acres, the pulse of an ethereal hush perpetuated itself beneath the canopied oaks, taking wing to soar into her heart and mind. It comforted her, much like fond memories from a gentler time. Though it softened the harsh effects of her stressful life, it then by its very nature birthed a deeper question. A question that was as old as mankind.

DR. JOHN ADAMS COMMANDED THE attention of those gathered for the service. With a Bible balanced in his large, weathered hands, he gazed into the distance, above those who dwelt on the emptiness of death. His thick, white hair ruffled in the morning breeze and compassion fit comfortably on his face.

Adams's deep baritone rumbled with emotion. Emotion that eulogized love for Paul Whittington. He closed his Bible and spoke softly to the hearts of those who grieved. His words addressed their eternal question. "In the wake of death, are we left with spiritual poverty? Are grief and despair our bitter companions?"

Adams's lined face softened when he lifted his hand. "Do you see only the husk of Paul Whittington and nothing more?"

In a moment of contemplation, he surveyed those present. "If you truly grieve for Paul, you will be consoled. For God has said, 'love those around you as you love yourself,' and from that action, He will comfort each and prepare the seeds of truth."

Adams narrowed his eyes. "The coldness of death appears so final, so complete. It's hard to see the purpose beyond. In nature, the seasons have their mission and tread in orderly fashion. Spring gives birth to life anew and passes to the majesty of summer's glory. Fall gives rise to impending change, allowing nature to ponder its path. And, in barren winter, there slumbers that frigid matron whose dreams clothe the fields in white.

"Yet, after the harshness of winter, the coming of life appears once more. Do we doubt or question this natural cycle? Certainly not. Like the coming of spring, God prepares our own regeneration. He who is eternal gave each person a part of his immortal self, and it follows that death is not final.

"But in the moment of our grief, do we question this truth? If you have ever pondered the vastness of our universe or contemplated the uniqueness of a rose, you realize a force behind reality. If you listen to the still, small voice within, the complexities and pain disappear. When you do, you open to the knowledge that transcends death. You glimpse a purpose beyond this realm. Your eyes open to the mysteries of the soul, and you experience God's love.

"Grief is a product of pain and blinds us to the beauty of His plan. For in the seasons of life, there is purpose behind the pattern. When our soul is immortal, our path but a circle, do you see an end?"

With the sweep of his hand, he summoned those to listen, and his vibrant message carried to where Sherry stood.

THE PAST FEW DAYS HAD been a difficult transition for Sherry since her grandfather's death. Even though she had constantly been near him in the hospice—and known the end was near—nothing prepared her for the emptiness she now felt. Dr. Adams's eulogy was comforting, yet she didn't care for his new age spirituality.

Grandfather had been unique in his religious beliefs too. From an early age, he'd studied the readings of a mid-1800's Christian mystic, Paul Stanley, who embraced the doctrine of reincarnation. However, living in the conservative realm of the Baptist stronghold, Grandfather had carefully hidden his true convictions. Until he met Dr. John Adams.

Adams's past was as interesting as the man himself. Thirty-five years ago, he graduated with a Doctorate in Divinity from Harvard. He possessed a spirit of questioning and the religious values that once comforted him came under relentless scrutiny. Having grown up in the Bible Belt too, John Adams knew where not to look for spiritual answers. He spent years wandering the west and east coasts, exposing himself to the isms and schisms of the religious world. After years of disappointment, John Adams came across the same Christian mystic, Paul Stanley, who had given a number of profound spiritual readings on a variety of topics. The bells that triggered Adams's interest were the readings on the nature of man's suffering.

To him, mainstream Christianity did not connect in why bad things happened to good people. He felt that some rain must fall in everyone's life, that the storm could be overcome, leaving one stronger. But he wondered about the purpose of disaster when it came in heavy portions.

Adams couldn't explain why a benevolent Father would afflict his children with such calamity. Yet when he studied Stanley's readings, something fell into place. The psychic did not espouse a new religion, for he embraced mainstream Christianity. When he entered a deep meditative state, he connected with a higher spiritual authority—one who offered enlightenment on a variety of topics, one of which included reincarnation.

Adams was overcome by the spirit of the readings, for they spoke to him on the deepest of levels. Hungrily devouring this spiritual information, the minister had reached a turning point in his life. The teachings of Christianity were still the foundation for his belief, but reincarnation became the vehicle to explain the excessive tribulation some face. For sins sown in past lives will ultimately be faced in the moment of now. The meeting of selves often brought intense suffering.

Sherry had heard Adams's story many times and was well acquainted with the minister from his visits with Grandfather. Despite Grandfather's earnest plea to accept Adams, she held the minister's beliefs as spiritual desecration.

Grandfather had donated generously to Adams's ministry, helping create a spiritual fountainhead of new age religion. Adams's renaissance boasted a cutting-edge sanctuary located in the Texas foothills of the majestic Palo Duro Canyon. From this stronghold, Adams inundated the airwaves with televised services that attracted hundreds of converts each week.

Sherry was aware of the provision in Grandfather's will bequeathing the church a generous annuity. While Dr. John Adams still lived, his church received one million dollars a year. Grandfather had placed a high value on his personal spirituality, as well as the friendship Adams bestowed.

From her vantage point behind the tree, she observed the lowering of the casket into the earth. Well-wishers stood and mingled with her mother, Sabra, pointing in Sherry's direction.

Embarrassed by the attention, Sherry stepped out of sight behind a huge oak tree. The wind eddied in uneasy currents and she leaned into the trunk, pressing her body against the rough bark. Beneath the tree's restless canopy, she fought the twisted demon of loss. Even though she'd experienced the spiritual beauty of Grandfather's passing, the strength of that occasion eroded in the face of grief. Loss over Grandfather and the walls of her mother's rejection soiled the spiritual tapestry. Bitter pain spread slowly, seeping through her gut and searing her heart.

Off in the distance, a low rumble of thunder rose in intensity, and while the sound of starting engines drifted across the cemetery, Sherry bowed her head and cried. Tears fell in testament to a bitter spiral, for the two people she loved most were lost to her.

"Sherry?"

The voice was edgy, hard, and masculine. Through tear-filled eyes, she recognized Cadence McShane. Wiping her eyes, she stammered, "Oh, I...." But the effort to regain her composure failed when he opened his arms. Like a child reaching for its parent, she accepted the comfort of his gesture.

He murmured, "We all feel the loss, Sherry."

Sherry stayed within his embrace, allowing Cadence to rock her while she grieved. The sound of departing limousines covered her cries as he stroked her hair.

The trembling finally subsided, and Sherry looked up. Tears ran down her cheeks. "I'm sorry."

"Don't be," Cadence released her and stepped back. Offering a clean bandana, he spoke in a husky voice. "You needed to cry."

As she took the cloth and dried her face, Cadence crossed his arms. Looking in the distance, calmness showed upon his face. "I wanted to offer my respect for your grandfather. Paul was genuine and took care of people 'round him. I only supervised his drillin' crew for a while, but he still treated me as an equal. In the world of haves and have nots, that's rare." He shifted his stance and looked in Sherry's eyes. "I understand how it feels to lose someone special. My brother died and we were real close. It's been seven years and I still miss him."

Cadence touched the back of her hand and she met his gaze. "If you'd like to talk, I'll be at the ranch."

His voice carried an unexpected tone of caring, and a blush warmed her cheeks. The sensitivity touched her deeply. "I wouldn't know where to start."

He turned her hand over and took the bandana. "Anywhere would be fine."

His long, thick fingers rested under hers and his sincerity created a bittersweet emotion inside Sherry, for his concern spoke of caring and emphasized its absence in her life.

Cadence withdrew the bandana, and the edge of her lips lifted in a shy smile. Words formed on her tongue just as footsteps came their way.

They both turned and watched a hundred pounds of spit and attitude storm toward them.

Dressed in a black, form-fitting Dior suit, Sabra Whittington planted her hands on her hips and stomped her booted foot on the grass. "Why are you hiding? Are you too good for the service?" Sabra thrust her face forward and screamed, "Where is your respect? Hiding behind a tree. Do you have any idea what my friends are saying?"

Cadence clenched his teeth and nodded at Sherry. "My condolences." To

Sabra, he curtly acknowledged her with a cold glare, and added, "You should have more respect for the grief of others."

Sabra's face turned unnaturally white, and her eyes narrowed into angry slits of cobalt blue. Distaste twisted her face as she watched Cadence walk away. She lifted her head and glared at Sherry. "I thought you made better choices in men. Daddy left you that worthless section of land and one drilling rig. Isn't that pretty? You're his boss now, and your toy won't have a reason to reject you." Sabra gripped Sherry's face and moved to within inches of her. "You listen," she spewed, "Your fantasy illness has no place in my life."

The emotional hostility damaged Sherry more than a physical blow.

Sabra glared at her with scorn. "If your father was here, he'd open his Bible and drive the devil from you. Hereditary mental illness? More like spiteful sin."

In the distance, jagged edges of lightning convulsed across the prairie and muted explosions rolled from dark, swollen clouds. Sherry clenched her fists and shook with silent pain.

"If you think you're coming back to this family, forget it." Sabra's last words rang with finality. She tilted her head. Smiled without warmth. Turned on her booted heel and stomped away.

Pain exploded across Sherry's chest, and reality forced the breath from her lungs. With this final act, she was now a voyeur to the memory of Sabra's love.

T-SHIRTS AT THE SPHINX

FOR EVERY FORCE, THERE IS an opposing force and the goodness in man is not complete without its opposite of evil. Yet, of all God's creatures, man was given free will to make his choices, and tonight, the thin membrane holding darkness in check was aborted, freed from the confines of its cell. Two men consciously raped that spiritual balance, and light succumbed to the darkness, malignancy vomited forth. Unseen evil throbbed in anticipation as Fat Boy's silenced semi-automatic popped. The gun's jagged flame violated the desert night, and invisible arms embraced the soul of John Davis. The twenty-year-old University of Texas student hit the desert floor, yards from his dead friends and the paws of the Egyptian Sphinx.

The Skeleton sucked on his cigarette and whispered, "Take his shirt, Fat Boy. My niece is a University of Texas fan."

"This has brains on it, too."

Standing seven feet tall and weighing 130 pounds, Skeleton flipped his cigarette in Fat Boy's face, littering sparks across the Egyptian night. "My niece wants a shirt. Why do you fuck up things, camel turd?" He motioned toward the last bound and gagged student. "How hard can it be?"

Fat Boy murmured, "Skeleton call me turd?" He turned and pulled the trigger three times, punching holes in the last student's T-shirt, and softly replied, "You'll have to buy her one now."

HIDDEN BEHIND THE RIGHT PAW of the Sphinx, Dr. Chuck Sandefur trembled while he watched his final team member die. The obese professor took his glasses off and wiped sweat from his eyes. Staring at his own UT shirt he thought, who the hell are these freaks?

This abortion of an archaeological project started one week ago, just two days after his fortieth birthday. The Office of Egyptian Antiquities invited him to conduct an unusual project at the Sphinx. In a curious move, they specifically asked for Chuck, an obscure University of Texas archeologist, to conduct comprehensive tests of the ancient monument to dispel the possibility of hidden compartments within the Sphinx or tunnels around it.

Chuck gathered a handful of bright UT students to conduct the grunt work, and left the electrified atmosphere of Austin, Texas, for Cairo, Egypt. The brutal desert sun couldn't dampen their spirits as Chuck and his five team members conducted exhaustive tests with sophisticated equipment, passing electrical currents through the Sphinx to locate hidden chambers, then taking traditional soundings of the surrounding limestone floor to locate tunnels.

But the results were depressing. There were no passages or undiscovered chambers. That is, until Chuck relied on his gut. "What if," he had asked the team, "someone built a tunnel impervious to traditional ground radar? What if the ancients had 'stealth' technology, either by chance or design?"

The five men were thoughtful and rallied by opening more beer. Seizing upon the possibility with alcohol-induced simplicity, they reasoned if there was an underground tunnel, there would be an entrance, so why not drive two-foot screws into the limestone floor and use an A-frame to hoist the entrance stone?

Since the official presence from the Egyptian Bureau of Antiquities, Simon Mohammed, had left for the day, they managed to drive three massive screws into the limestone in unsuccessful attempts to find the opening. Darkness fell, and the sweating men drove a fourth screw into the bedrock near the right paw of the Sphinx. Three students strained on the overhead winch, desperate to hoist the stone, but nothing moved.

Tipping the scale at three hundred pounds, Chuck grabbed the end of the lever and pulled with the others. The rapidly cooling desert assaulted their sweating bodies, creating a chilling shock, sending energy through their systems. Renewing their downward pressure, an agonizing screech of stone against stone pierced the night, and archaeological history wrote itself. Stone wrenched from its placement, and an ancient tunnel opened before them, exposing a shimmering, blue liquid floating just below the entrance.

The men stood in awe-struck silence and Chuck nonchalantly drained his beer. With a straight face, he said, "We'll check it after I pee." He belched and waddled behind the Sphinx's right paw.

That had been fifteen minutes ago and five murders later. Now, Chuck stood quietly in a puddle of urine, hidden from the assassins. Peering around the paw, he saw a Middle Eastern Abbott and Costello walk toward the shimmering blue light.

Chuck gripped his pocket crucifix and choked with rage. He studied the men while they stood before the tunnel entrance, noting their features for identification. *Damn it,* Chuck thought, *I'm outnumbered, outgunned, but not out of luck.* With a backwards glance, he observed the ladder leaning against the base of the Sphinx's right paw.

He padded quietly to the ladder and put his prosthetic left leg on the first rung. Sand and limestone crunched beneath, even though he moved with quiet intensity, rising one step at a time. The archeologist took a deep breath, gritted his teeth and lumbered on to the back of the Sphinx's paw.

Standing eight feet above the limestone floor, Chuck said a prayer and asked God to give him guidance.

With their backs to the Sphinx, Abbott and Costello bent at their waists, peering into the blue, metallic liquid. Skeleton whispered, "It is so strange." He poked his hand in and pulled it out. "There's an opening beneath."

Chuck focused on the assassins and crept silently forward. He took one step at a time, hoping his luck would hold. But, two feet from the end of the paw, his Reebok scraped the coarse, weathered stone. He halted in the darkness and held his breath, hoping the men had not heard. His heart pounded so hard it hurt. Behind closed eyes, flashes of light arced in the darkness. Time stood still, and Chuck opened his eyes. On the edge of the flickering blue light, he stood frozen. The surrounding desert was totally dark, and the lights of Cairo glowed against the low hanging clouds. To his right, five dead friends lay on the sand.

Silently, Chuck edged to the end of the paw and realized he didn't have a clue what to do. Standing well above the heads of the assassins, he swayed with uncertainty.

The two men turned around.

Chuck's moment had come.

Fat Boy grinned, pulling lips back to expose rotting teeth. He glanced at Skeleton. "Here's your niece's shirt, camel turd." In a heartbeat, he jerked the gun up and shot Chuck in the face.

The bullet skimmed along the fleshy part of the archeologist's cheek, and he screamed in rage. Survival kicked in and he jumped into space, dropping three hundred pounds of retribution on the bastard's heads.

Like a slow-motion film, he fell. Cool wind flowed across his face, and Fat Boy's rotting teeth were so close, he could smell the decay. To his left, perspiration trickled down Skeleton's forehead and fear darkened the man's eyes.

The metallic blue of the floating liquid deepened in color and a strange, humming sound came from below.

Fat Boy pointed the gun and fired again, but the shot went high, into the desert.

The slow motion stopped. Chuck's massive stomach smashed Skeleton's head, twisting his neck backward, bending the bone unnaturally. A sickening pop left the murderer dead.

Fat Boy tried to put his hands up to push Chuck away, but the weight was too great, and he crumpled to the ground.

Lying on top of the two men, Chuck screamed, "Take that, you son of a bitch," and pounded a massive fist into Fat Boy's windpipe.

Oblivious to the damage, Fat Boy swung his pistol, whipping Chuck's temple and ripping the skin.

Stunned, but not out of commission, Chuck operated on instinct. He jerked his shirt up and writhed toward Fat Boy's face. With his right hand, he clamped the assassin's gun hand and secured the other in a sweaty grip.

Fat Boy jerked his knee upward, smashing Chuck's balls.

Pain knifed through his gut and he almost let go, but adrenaline kicked in and Chuck regained his grip on the assassin's hands. He inched his massive stomach toward Fat Boy's face, where layers of fat formed an airtight seal over the murderer's mouth and nose, restricting his air and smothering him with pounds of soft, human flesh.

Like an animal held under water, Fat Boy jerked and bucked, frantic to dislodge Chuck. Thrashing his legs, he kicked again and again, trying to get air.

One minute passed and Fat Boy still rocked and jerked and thrashed, unwilling to die. He fought against the pressure on his gun hand, squeezed the trigger five times, sending bullets into the desert floor.

Sweat ran down Chuck's back and the layers of fat that covered Fat Boy's face. His death grip on the assassin's hands remained firm, and he had moved his crotch away from the flailing legs.

From beneath his stomach, Fat Boy began to bite and shred the flesh, causing blood to ooze to the sand.

Chuck screamed in rage and forced his body harder against the murderer.

In one final effort, Fat Boy jerked, legs thrashing and body quivering. Then he went limp.

The archaeologist slowly counted to sixty before rolling off.

He lay on the desert sand, panting from the pain, staring at the stars. His heart raced so hard he thought he might die, but as the minutes passed, his rhythm subsided and he breathed easier. With a deep sigh he said thanks to God. But lying there on the ground, he began to shake. Tears dropped like rain and a low intimate laugh started. He shook so hard his entire body jiggled. Looking over his massive stomach, he said to the dead men, "Thank you McDonalds, for all those Happy Meals."

Lying on his back, the night air felt good, but after a few minutes he gradually sat up. Chuck pulled his UT shirt down, and the cotton absorbed the blood when he pressed it against his torn flesh. Gingerly touching his temple and cheek, he knew he would live. Yet in a moment of dark insight, he realized whatever was in the tunnel was worth killing for.

He got to his feet and staggered to the metal ladder. His arms trembled too much to pick it up, so he dragged it to the tunnel opening. Lowering it into the square hole, the ten-foot ladder hit solid ground. Chuck looked at the floating blue liquid and bent over. He cautiously touched the luminous substance and felt neither wetness nor warmth. It offered no resistance as he pushed downward into the tunnel, and like water, it formed around his arm. Chuck moved his hand below the blue veil and came in contact with the tunnel wall, which dropped straight down. He pulled out of the liquid and tried to splash it, hoping to glimpse what lay beneath, but it was like trying to separate a solid substance. Curiously, it was liquid, yet had properties of a solid. It could be penetrated with direct force but could not be divided with angular pressure.

Basic instinct gnawed inside—call the authorities—but it was replaced by an equally strong desire to see what was there. Chuck gripped the top rung and slowly descended into the blue liquid. With increasing tension, he stepped into the greatest mystery of his life.

TUNNEL OF
SECRETS

CHUCK DESCENDED INTO THE LIQUID, pausing as it came to his chin. Closing his eyes, he took a deep breath and moved onto the tunnel floor. He thought the floating substance was only a few inches thick, but it could fill the underground passage. Panic knotted his gut as he held his breath.

He cautiously opened his eyes and looked upward to see that the floating liquid extended six inches downward from the opening. It was safe to breathe, so he took one step into the dark. When he did so, a strange sensation flowed over him—like he'd stepped through a thin membrane, as if passing through the subtle resistance of a spider's web. In response, a faint luminescence sparkled around his feet, sending out spider webs of tiny electric charges. Like a catalyst in a chemical reaction, it spawned scores of similar veins, electric tendrils, and crab-like wisps of energy that shot outward, creating an eerie light.

The spider web grew exponentially, cascading across the floor, up both sides, and onto the ceiling above. It rippled fifteen yards down the tunnel into what looked like a small circular chamber. Similar to turning on rows of fluorescent lights one at a time, the passage illuminated in three segments of electric white, then morphed to cobalt blue.

A few wisps of veined electricity sputtered and dissipated from view.

What had he walked into?

He moved down the tunnel, curious about the fresh, clean air. Placing his hand on the wall, a white aura formed around it, then faded when he walked into the circular chamber. The floor felt padded, like walking on foam, so he stomped his foot, and surprisingly, no sound came from the impact.

He focused on the center of the chamber, and the breath jolted from his lungs. A human-sized crystal skull floated three feet above the floor. Unbelievably articulated, it was the most accurate reproduction he'd ever seen. Blue points of light winked and flickered within the empty eye sockets as Chuck moved closer. He passed his hand around it to detect supporting wires or a harness and found none. But the mystery deepened when he touched the top of the crystal surface. The skull opened into two halves just above the brows and revealed two hand impressions.

He was out of his league, so he did the obvious thing. He put his hands in the indentations.

The chamber wall's dark liquid covering turned into pure, white energy, bathing him in unspoiled brilliance. It quickly faded to midnight blue, and an image appeared on the shimmering liquid. Chuck recognized a five-year-old boy with tousled brown hair. By some incredible mechanism, he was a voyeur to his past. Young Chuck stood next to his mother's bed, placing a tray of scrambled eggs, burnt toast, and juice on her lap. The boy grinned, exposing two missing front teeth, and adjusted his superman cape. "Mommy, eat your food, take your vitamins, and you'll get better." Little Chuck reached over and put a napkin on the tray. He picked up a Flintstone vitamin and scrunched his face. "This one's Fred." Chuck gave a lopsided grin. "He's better than Dino cause Dino's just a dog. Dogs don't know nothin' about getting better." He grabbed another vitamin in his tiny hand, "If Fred won't get you unsick, Barney'll do the job."

Momma Sandefur lay on her pillow, holding her small cross. Her face was twisted from pain, yet she coaxed a tired smile.

Chuck looked up. "When I told Joey you had canker, he said put Blistex on it, and it'll go away." He smiled and put the small tube next to her. "Joey's ten an' knows everything."

Momma put her trembling hand under Chuck's chin and adjusted her sleeve to hide the brownish-black skin. The left side of her neck and face were tainted with ugly, dark splotches, yet concern shone in her eyes. "I love you, Chuck." She spoke each word slowly and tenderly, her fingers lingering beneath his jaw.

"I love you, too, Momma." Chuck fidgeted with his cape and moved closer. "Are you gonna be with Jesus?"

A single tear came to her eye, and Chuck reached up, gently wiping it away. Her voice trembled. "Soon, sweetie."

"Don't worry. I had a dream last night. We were with Jesus and I asked if I could come with you. He told me no, because I still had some 'portant work to do." Chuck bowed his head and took his Mother's hand. "He said God watches over us. Do you believe that, Momma?"

With waning strength, she whispered, "More than you know, honey. More than you'll ever know." She moved her fingers from under Chuck's chin and beckoned him closer. Pressing the small cross into his palm, she kissed his head. "Promise me something?"

Chuck's eyes opened wide.

"When I'm gone, look for the good in people and help those in need. Be kind to everyone you meet."

He closed his fingers around the crucifix. "You mean do what I'm doin' now." There was no question in his voice.

"Yes, I do."

THE ARCHAEOLOGIST WIPED HIS EYES and watched the image fade, yet more history burst upon the screen showing the spiritual tapestry of his life. True to his promise, he had given years of altruistic service with unselfish acts of the heart, words of encouragement and kindness. Yet stranger than this astounding montage, Chuck felt what the people felt. Every kind act he'd ever done had an effect upon the recipient, and Chuck reeled when he connected to each person's experience. Tapping into an unknown realm, he profoundly felt each person's happiness and gratitude.

In a twisted dichotomy, Chuck faced his analytical mind and the sheer insanity of this setting. For the first time in his life, he doubted the foundation that he'd used. He questioned the scientific mind. This was not to say logic and reason didn't have a place, but he realized there was another realm that we're not aware of, a cavern of deeper insight and truth. How could images of his past play in a mysterious chamber under the Egyptian sands? What sort of mechanism took the focal point of his spiritual tapestry and played it back in such a manner that he actually felt the emotions of others?

Somewhere in the back of his mind, Chuck knew there was more than logic and science, yet stepping into the area of mysticism frightened him. His tool had always been the rational mind, so if you couldn't use logic to reason and solve, then it was better to leave the unknown alone. His world of science and stability bowed to the sheer force of the enigma on the screen and he marveled at the world of sacred insight. It flashed upon him that the important things in life are not how much money you make or what you attain, but rather how much you care for others. Thoughtfulness, smiles of encouragement, and kind words were the coin of this realm.

A subtle bliss settled in his mind, and he knew himself to be the same, yet everything had changed.

Thirty-five years of history ended, and Chuck looked at his watch. Incredibly, only two minutes had passed. Somehow, in that fleeting space of time, the obligation made to his mother had played itself out, defining the path he had followed. As a man of singular faith, he knew things happened for a purpose. The sudden epiphany hit full force. His spirituality was the key to this momentous discovery. Somehow, some way, it made sense.

"How utterly sublime," came a feminine voice from behind.

Chuck turned and faced a woman, standing with long legs apart and wearing a blond wig. Her small breasts pushed against black spandex, and she gripped a wicked semi-automatic in her left hand.

"Who are you?" whispered Chuck.

"Morda."

The first round took Chuck in the left kneecap, and three more penetrated his upper thigh. He hit the ground, screaming horrifically, paralyzing his vocal cords with the strain. Air rushed from his lungs and filled the chamber with his pain. He writhed on the floor and blood saturated his pant leg.

Morda stood over him and smiled.

To the left, the crystal skull closed, and a thin stream of blue liquid started draining from the walls and flowing from the floor up to the crystal. In a prophetic tone, the last image on the circular screen showed Chuck lying motionless upon the ground.

Morda flipped her long blond hair back. "You'll go into shock and bleed out soon, so enjoy life. What's left of it."

Chuck twitched and gasped erratically for several minutes. Finally, he lay still.

As the last of the metallic liquid receded into the skull, it slowly lowered to the dirt. In the ensuing darkness, Morda broke the glass in two chemical lights and threw one next to Chuck. She sneered at him, put the skull in a cloth sack, and left.

Eerie fluorescence bathed the chamber, outlining Chuck's body against the wall. One minute crept by. Silence as deep as a mausoleum filled the chamber, and then Chuck gasped for air.

Sitting up, he carefully felt his shattered leg, the prosthetic one that went to mid-thigh. Getting out his pocket knife, he cut the pant leg off and formed the material in to a bandage. The one bullet wound to the lower stump of his leg was messy and he realized it was only a flesh wound. Thankful the deception had worked, Chuck pulled himself across the dusty floor. Straining from the exertion, it took thirty minutes to move down the tunnel to the entrance. The ladder was gone. Chuck looked at his watch. In eight hours, the Egyptian Antiquities official would show up. The makeshift bandage was holding, yet blood continued to ooze. He leaned against the wall and reached for his cross. Closing his eyes, he prayed Simon would be early for a change.

ROAD TO HELL

SHERRY POPPED THE CLUTCH AND the motorcycle shrieked with raw power, smoking the rear tire. A whitish, blue cloud boiled off the apartment complex's parking lot and the Beemer fishtailed as it rocketed onto the highway.

Pulling her Ray Bans down, she was thankful her visions never occurred while driving. With the sun upon her face, she slammed through the gears to fifth, keeping the speed legal until she hit the Road to Hell.

The 600 cc five-hundred pound Beemer gripped the pavement with un-believable stability, and the barren Texas landscape blurred when Sherry hit seventy miles per hour. And what no sane BMW mechanic would do, her part-ner-in-crime did. Lightfeather bolted a pressurized, steel container of nitrous oxide to the rear luggage rack and connected lines to each Bing carburetor, supercharging the bike and extending its speed into the realm of insanity.

Hot, dry wind flowed around the fairing, cocooning her in dead air. On the way to Grandfather's ranch lay a stretch of sun-baked, desolate road. The Cat Eye radar detector was silent, and she shifted in the saddle, anticipating the G-force.

Twenty miles of tribulation lay between Sherry and her father's memory, and the very thought of him brought bile to her mouth. Festering anger erupt-ed, and she mashed the nitrous switch. Twisting the throttle hard, unbelievable acceleration kicked like a blow to her chest. The skin on her face wrinkled from the instant G-force, and the speedometer jumped from 70 to 110. The engine screamed in mortal agony, and roadside fence posts turned into gray smudges. With a small grin, she screamed, *"Blow,* you son-of-a-bitch!"

SHERRY ALWAYS TRIED TO RELIVE the last memory of her father from his point of view to understand his actions, and that memory always started with the tent. The big canvas one, like at the circus. Its white material curved upward, like the belly of a dead, bloated cow as it rested in Paul Whittington's pasture. The huge structure lay one mile east of Amarillo and a quarter mile off the State road. Despite the fanatical grip of a hot autumn night, the crowd came early, raising layers of fine Texas dust while gleaming Chevys and Fords roared up the serpentine path for a date with Brother 'Hell' Whittington. The enormous tent's sides were pulled back and worn benches, ten feet long, were placed on either side of a sawdust path leading to the podium. From this epicenter of hellfire and brimstone, Brother Hell kneaded strong men and women into malleable clay, baptizing them in the fear of God. Under the curved canvas above, rows of electric lights dangled like Christmas decorations, creating an undercurrent of excitement among the growing crowd.

More vehicles sped across the dry, dead field to disgorge spiritual thrill seekers intent upon an emotional roller-coaster ride.

At the end of the tent, just beyond the podium, Brother Hell sat in his 1970 Cadillac, smoking a Lucky Strike and enjoying the last minutes of air-conditioned comfort. He took a final pull on the pint of Jim Beam and tucked the empty under the seat with the others. He turned to his twelve-year-old daughter, Sherry, who stared sullenly at her lap, avoiding his eyes.

He crushed the cigarette in an ashtray overloaded with butts and gripped her arm. "You come when I call. I won't tolerate no disobedience."

She pressed the white cotton gown against her thin legs and spoke to the dusty dash, "I won't make you mad, Daddy."

"Make damn sure you don't." He glanced at the tent and an usher waved him on to the podium. It was time, and Brother Hell knew souls needed saving tonight. He took a deep breath and felt mean and hungry. It was all in the name of God. He liked the edge it gave, knew he couldn't live without it. That hunger put him in the spirit to preach, to lead the sheep to the path of redemption. Sins of transgression and laziness whetted his need, and his hunger demanded more each time he fed upon their fear. All sins would be dealt with harshly, but tonight would be special. He'd come to serve notice on the Devil. Look the bastard in the eye. Fight fire with fire.

He glanced at Sherry and left the car, taking long strides to the platform and its center. His black, satin suit shimmered under the sixty-watt bulbs. He removed his handkerchief, mopping the sweat upon his brow.

Some women called him handsome, tall and lean, with dark brown hair. Yet those who knew him were cowed by his intensity, fearful of that glint in his eyes. Brother Hell intimidated and mesmerized, pulled no punches, and his righteous anger whipped the sheep into a frenzy. He nurtured the fertile ground of fear, guilting his flock, then offering salvation with a trip down the aisle. There wasn't anything he couldn't do, and he didn't give a damn what anyone thought. The sheep out there belonged to him and he had no mercy. Not before, and particularly not tonight.

The tent bulged with four-hundred men, women, and children. Late comers stood in the aisle, and others jostled around the tent's edge hoping to view the preacher.

Brother Hell addressed the crowd with a simple gesture, raising his right hand, beckoning them to stand. After the sound of hundreds rising to their feet, there was a hush so quiet, so profound, he could hear them listening. Waiting for the Word—anything to change their pathetic lives. There, in the tinsel glow of dim bulbs, hundreds looked up. At him, Brother Hell. Not a whisper of wind touched the tent, and through the open canvas flaps, choked starlight flickered in a background of utter darkness.

Caught in the moment of now, Brother Hell focused on something deep and far away, his own private realm, his fearsome reservoir of power. The words unfolded in his mind, and he spoke without aid of a microphone, projecting to the edge of the tent. The crowd leaned forward when he asked, "Can ya feel it?" Touching the handkerchief to his lips, he smelled the good Southern bourbon.

The fire flared in his gut, and he ached deep inside. He spoke a little louder, "People, can ya feel it?"

A few soft "Amens" were uttered from the crowd. Someone in the back cried, "Down with Satan."

In a demanding voice, he bellowed, "Can ya feel it?" Brother Hell smacked his Bible and answered, "I can." He gestured to the right, "I feel it there and there." Bowing his head, prayer-like, he shook his Bible. "I feel the devil at work." People glanced at their friends and neighbors, and Brother Hell looked up and glared at them. He shouted, "The Beast is in your heart and feasts on your soul. His wickedness lives." He put a finger to his chest. "But tonight I will defeat him. For I am the fist of God."

The crowd rallied with foot stomping and cheers.

"No one's safe. Not you, not even me." He lifted his head, and even those in the back heard him clearly. "I have a confession." The good Brother turned to the side, giving his best profile. "The Devil is a coward and will not attack me. But the damned Serpent has a grip on someone dear. One close to my heart." With a grand motion, he waved Sherry to the stage.

Walking on bare feet across the dirt, Sherry trembled as she moved up to the podium.

Towering over his daughter, Brother Hell shepherded her to a round, galvanized stock tank. Dried moss stuck to the inside of the steel and the cloudy, tepid water was two feet deep, just inches below the rim.

The good Brother looked upon Sherry and his lips turned into a thin, cruel smile.

His daughter whimpered.

He ignored her and screamed, "The devil has my baby. Satan feasts on her soul."

A chorus of "Death to Satan," rocked the tent, and Sherry flinched when her father touched her.

"No one is free from Satan, not even my child." He gave his most solemn look and stepped into the tank. Bending over, he placed his Bible on the ground and lifted Sherry over the edge. "Sweet Jesus. What has the Devil done? I'll tell you, Lucifer puts pictures in her mind."

The crowd exploded with thunderous shock and cried, "God is King. Save her Brother."

The preacher turned his eyes upward and shouted, "Why would Satan possess this child? Because he's a coward and chooses the weak. But tonight, my baby will come to Jesus."

He put his left hand under her neck and placed the sweaty handkerchief over her mouth. Pinching her nostrils shut, he lowered her into the water and commanded, "Almighty Jesus, chase Satan from my child." Brother Hell lifted her up and proclaimed, "She is on the Road to Hell. Sweet Lord, bring her back."

Angry cries pierced the night, and scores talked in tongues. Women clasped their babies, and men shook their fists. Pandemonium reigned while the people chanted, "Drown the Devil!"

Brother Hell felt the eyes upon him when he pushed Sherry down again into the brackish water and jerked her up. He sucked the energy of four hundred people as they beseeched a vengeful God to drive Satan from his girl.

Sherry's hair lay plastered on her face, and she rubbed silt from her eyes. The white gown clung to her twelve-year-old body, outlining thin arms and legs.

Brother Hell commanded, "Pray with me." He put his hands upon her head and challenged the crowd, "Most merciful Lord, drive the darkness out."

Hundreds swayed, and the spirit possessed their souls, commanding their bodies to twist and writhe, unknowingly paying homage to the power of Brother Hell. Grown men cried and young children danced in the dirt, jerking with bastard rhythm.

Brother Hell hungered, imbibed on absolute domination, and coasted on the crest of power and control. Until he glanced down. He jerked back in outrage. The blood drained from his face, and his thoughts turned cold and violent. He strangled the words, "Oh, God."

The crowd still writhed like a headless snake, unaware that something had gone wrong. Bad wrong.

Brother Hell raised his fist and screamed at his daughter, "Goddammit, what have you done."

Sherry turned and faced her Father. Flinching from the anger in his voice, she put her arms up to protect her face.

And like a ripple effect, the people in the front rows stared, and those behind did, too, until finally, four hundred people reeled in shock. With her back to the crowd, a trail of blood blossomed from Sherry's panties, spreading across the white gown, staining crimson down her thighs.

She looked up at her father and cried, "What's happening?"

SHERRY STILL MASHED THE NITROUS button, and two miles of road disappeared in fifty seconds. The engine wailed in protest as a quarter ton of machinery rocketed down the hot, narrow road. At 120 mph everything emptied from her mind while the BMW devoured the Road to Hell.

But the little girl inside her always asked, "Why? Why did he leave? Why didn't he ever come back?"

She didn't have the answer.

This motorcycle had been Daddy's joy and was the remaining link between her and her father. For the last twenty-one years, she had tried to trash it. Destroy what it stood for.

But, like it had for all these years, the engine refused to blow. And the twenty miles of tribulation lead back to where it all began. Nothing had changed. Once more, in the grip of defeat, she cut the speed and hung her head. Bitter tears fell, and Sherry realized that the demons she tried hardest to kill just refused to die.

WHO THE HELL ARE YOU?

DEEP IN THE TEXAS PRAIRIE, an emerging hush consumed Sherry as she coasted into Grandfather's ranch. Autumn wings had unfolded to shower the land with endless hues of brown and gold, creating a majestic beauty.

Coming to a stop at the edge of the driveway, she cut the engine and put the bike on its stand.

The cool afternoon breeze brought the smell of oil and gasoline when Lightfeather stepped out of the workshop.

"I suppose you'll trash the engine tomorrow?" he said, referring to the still operating motorcycle.

"Yep," she nodded her head. "Got to one-twenty before it leveled out. Can you tweak the carbs for more speed?"

"Been tweaking for twenty-one years." Lightfeather shaded his eyes from the pale fall sun. "What's a little more. Hmm?"

Sherry hung her head and stared at the asphalt. Without warning, the shadow of madness surged within. The familiar fear started in her gut, and sanity bled like it was slashed by razor wire.

Lightfeather casually wiped his hands on a shop rag. "Someone was asking about you earlier." He pointed to the pipe rack, where Cadence was welding, and looked back. Narrowing his eyes, Lightfeather scanned her face. "Are you okay?"

Forcing a bright smile, she kept eye contact, hoping to dispel Lightfeather's concern, but in her altered state of mind, reality slipped and she fell into a pit of mind-numbing fear. Outwardly, her face betrayed a fraction of the turmoil within, and she struggled in silence to fight the approaching jaws of insanity. By focusing on the road's crazy patchwork, Sherry tried to gain control. She attempted to force rational thought by envisioning what normal people might see. For some, the asphalt might present random lines, or varying shades of black and grey. For others, the patterns could take a benevolent shape. But in her private hell, the images formed a Devil's Rorschach where distorted faces and disturbing actions lay within a valley of evil so dark, her soul trembled. Sherry's mind conjured naked images of satanic faces and beast-like creatures. The acidic fear coated her perceptions, aborting her fragile state of mind.

Consumed by this horrible flow, she was powerless to stop it. Having learned from the perpetual, mind-numbing agony, she knew the process had to run its course. Sooner or later, it would bleed itself out.

Yet, in the midst of her torment, Sherry was strangely attuned to Lightfeather. He watched her closely.

In a detached manner, she studied the look upon his weathered face and knew he could read her expression. He was aware of her inner struggle but didn't have a clue of its horrible depth. In this forest of fear, schizophrenia was the hunter, and she, the fawn. With soul-wrenching frequency, the pattern played over and over. Defenseless against the brute power of skewed brain chemistry, sanity was ruptured by its action. Yet when someone sensed the subtle change in her face and wondered if something was wrong, Sherry would never tell them, for their illusions were kinder than the truth.

Mercifully, her focus changed, and control surged within. As quickly as it came, darkness lifted, yet pustules of fear remained. The transition to the dark side of madness repeatedly impaled her, and she had shared her inner turmoil only with Lightfeather. So, in a forced manner, she gave him an upbeat nod. "Know what?" she said.

"What?"

"I see a pattern in the road, something like… a skunk. Yea, Paula LePew." Pinching her nostrils, she rolled her eyes and said, "P U."

A sad look filled his face and he paused while considering his words. "How are you doing now?"

Sherry knew he perceived some of her inner trauma, for they had been friends all her life.

He had watched her grow and been a part of her life emotionally and spiritually. Yet, these schisms of reality happened all the time and she knew what his question referred to. She wanted to keep it silly and light, but Lightfeather deserved the truth. So, she confided, "I miss him terribly."

"Paul loved you, Sherry."

"I know he did." When Sherry thought of Grandfather, she glanced at her bracelet for the heart-shaped charm, a gift from him. "Oh, damn it."

"What's wrong?"

"The heart, it's gone." Shaking her head in disbelief, she cried, "He gave it to me when I was seven."

"I'm sure it'll show up where you least expect it."

"I hope so." Glancing over at Cadence, she moved closer to Lightfeather. "I need to talk. Is now a good time?" Dry wind eddied around them, whipping dust into tight knots. Sherry lowered her voice and touched his arm. "Some strange things have happened."

Lightfeather's long white hair moved in the breeze. "Like what?"

"I saw something the other day that bothered me. You know my hallucination, the one I've had all these years? It starts with the pumpkins and is in black and white. Ever since I was twelve, it's never changed. It still creeps me out."

"You've told me."

"Well, there's more. When I was with Grandfather and he was dying, I had the most incredible," she swallowed hard, "vision. But this time, it was in full color and had a message. It wasn't frightening, because it spoke with eloquence and power."

She related the details and watched Lightfeather. Not once did his face show doubt while he absorbed her story.

Contemplating, he stroked his chin. "What you've described is a spiritual awakening. The fact that it's benevolent and had a message is important." He tucked the shop rag in his pocket and crossed his arms. "As a young boy in

Mexico, I studied with a mystic priestess and experienced my own awakening." Lightfeather stood tall and proud yet spoke softly. "When the path has been shown, the journey starts with a single step."

"What am I supposed to do? Can you help?"

He pondered a moment. "My inner voice says I'm not the teacher. But I know someone who will guide you. Mr. Irby is his name."

"Wonderful. When can we go?"

Lightfeather looked at his watch. "I'll give him a call now, and we'll catch him before his nap."

"Great. But there's more to tell. Before Grandfather died, I went to a psychic and had another experience. When she gave my reading, I had my fingers against her palm. It was so eerie because a sensation of calm came over me, and then my mind exploded with images. Images of her lying to her clients. She fed on their pain and suffering and played upon their fear. Then she lied by saying horrible things would happen to their loved ones.

"And when the client was scared enough, she offered to stop the tragedy by praying to the angels. In every case, her intervention wasn't cheap, because she'd charge hundreds of dollars for her 'help.' Mother Sonja had a con going, because she took part of the truth and layered it with lies. The connection I forged showed her fraud, but how did it work?"

Lightfeather stared into the distance. "You accessed a psychic pathway or chakra. Ancient teaching says they're located around the body, with a minor one in each palm. If you're receptive, and touch someone's palm with your fingertips, you open a conduit to tune in to that person."

He furrowed his brow. "Suppose you have two identical tuning forks in a room, and when you strike one, it transmits a vibration. That energy travels to the other fork and starts it humming at the same frequency. Another example is two violins, both strung with the same length, thickness, and tautness of string. Pluck one violin string and the other will sing in tune with it. The same goes for people. The trick is being receptive to the other person's 'vibrations.' Animals and children are more open to this transference and have a natural ability." Lightfeather swept his hand across his forehead and moved his long hair away. "When I tune in to a person, I pick up and amplify what he 'feels' like. I open my mind to his vibrations and let them resonate within. When you allow this to happen, you'll see the images his mind dwells upon."

Lightfeather turned away from her. "Guess I'll go call Mr. Irby then tweak the carburetors. Before I forget, stay away from the septic tank. The ground's a little soft." Sherry watched Lightfeather walk away and was emotionally torn over her two visions. On one hand, they reverberated with truth, but her Fundamentalist indoctrination during childhood condemned them as evil.

A noise drew her attention to the workshop where Cadence was working with a welding rod. His presence struck a nerve that quickened her pulse. A pulse that jumped when she sensed his power and masculinity.

Cadence removed the welder's hood and swept shimmering, black hair behind his ear. Like a chameleon changing color, the facial components of his concentration faded, and a slow, confident smile emerged.

Seven determined strides brought him to Sherry's side, and he gently took her hand.

The ever-present breeze ruffled his dark hair. "I hope you're doin' better since the funeral."

She lost herself in his dark, brooding eyes, and his face filled with sincerity when she pressed her fingertips against his warm flesh. In the field around them, prairie grass rustled and bobwhites called across the open land.

Stillness came upon her and she was aware of her eyes shifting upward and to the left.

Sherry's fingertips vibrated with Cadence's distinct energy and the immense power of an image pressed upon her inner eye with a life of its own. In this vision, Cadence stood in crisp, khaki pants and starched shirt before a chalkboard with the words Joint CIA/FBI Remote Viewing Briefing. An audience of twelve grim-faced men stared back, waiting for instructions.

Cadence unfolded the paper in his hand and viewed a partial map of the East Coast. Where Washington, D.C. should have been, there was now a sixty-eight-mile radius of white, empty space. A crude hourglass and question mark were drawn, stating a premeditated threat.

No one in the intelligence community had known of the plot until the map was found stapled to the forehead of a ranking U.S. Middle Eastern diplomat. His staff, himself, and his family had been brutally slaughtered behind the secure doors of the American embassy in Saudi Arabia. The fact that the embassy's security had been breached so easily—as well as the sadistic presentation of the map—was not lost on higher ups. In an atmosphere of heightened anxiety, all intelligence sources were scrutinized and ruthlessly examined, but nothing showed in the network. As a final resort, desperate superiors employed the unorthodox, and reluctantly pressed for a joint CIA/FBI remote viewing team to find an answer.

Still connected with Cadence, his words flowed effortlessly into Sherry's mind. "Each team member will be given remote viewing targets. Now go to your controller and begin."

As the men left the room, Cadence's hands shook slightly, and his voice divulged fear he fought to control, "God help us. I hope we're not too late."

A vibrational charge surged through Sherry's fingertips, and the psychic connection severed. Letting go of Cadence's hand, the utter power of her vision filled her with inner dread. She'd had three psychic manifestations in one day, and if her parents were right, there was a special place in hell for her. But the undeniable force, the bone-shaking rightness of them, lent conviction to her paranormal perceptions.

Angry words bubbled inside her, addressing the truthfulness of Cadence's identity. But caution stilled her desire to speak. Sherry curled a strand of loose hair around her finger and gave him a soft smile. She looked deep into his eyes, and thought, Cadence McShane, just who the hell are you?

THE SCREEN DOOR SLAMMED BEHIND Sherry and she stepped into Lightfeather's house. Located twenty yards from the workshop, the ranch home consisted of an office, three sparsely furnished bedrooms, living room, small kitchen, and a shower and toilet.

Sherry sat at the office's computer and moved Lightfeather's 'borrowed' dish, which contained an eagle's feather and an arrowhead. Lightfeather had explained years ago, that whenever his Comanche Indian ancestors took something sacred from those outside of the tribe, they left the feather and carved arrowhead in acknowledgment. Kind of like a spiritual form of counting coup.

She placed the dish to the side, fired up the PC, and typed in *'remote viewing.'* The Google search got over eight million hits, so, she scanned the page and clicked, *'I'm feeling lucky.'* An online encyclopedia came up with a synopsis that piqued her interest. *"Remote viewing"* it read, *"is the purported ability for a viewer to gather information on a remote target consisting of an object, place, or person, etc., that is hidden from the physical perception of the viewer and typically separated from the viewer at some distance."* She read the various code names for the government's psychic spying program and learned the project was active from the 1970's to early 1994. It was an offshoot of research done at the Stanford Research Institute that went into military application—however, when the Cold War ended, the unit's end was in sight. It was turned over to the CIA in 1993 and later disbanded in 1994.

Even though she had felt guilty using her psychic connection with Cadence, the computer information screamed the obvious. The project was still thriving, even though the Agency officially started the closure after 'commissioning' two studies to do a retrospective evaluation of the unit's results. The CIA's choice of handpicked skeptics resulted in their recommendation to end the project.

Reading between the lines, the CIA had deflected public interest, yet allowed the project to operate covertly. Now there seemed to be a recent effort between the CIA and the FBI—i.e. Cadence McShane—to find the enemy behind a plot to destroy Washington, D.C.

A box popped up in the computer screen's right-hand corner and listed *Remote Viewing People,* so Sherry clicked on the name Ingo Swann. Swann, it stated, was an artist and psychic who'd helped develop the scientific process called Controlled Remote Viewing for the military. The declassified picture showed a group of people in civilian clothes who were trainees for the project. Looking closer, she guessed the date to be in the early seventies due to the men's hair styles and clothing.

Sherry clicked on several other names and shuffled through pictures of little interest. A final shot showed the CIA spokesperson announcing the closure of the Remote Viewing Unit in 1994. Twelve people sat at the table behind the podium, and she quickly scanned their faces. With her finger poised to close the screen, something caught her eye. The picture was small, so with a few clicks, Sherry enlarged it and focused on the face that caught her attention. A side view of a young man with light hair and strong features intrigued her. But, as she studied his countenance, something tugged within. Struggling for recognition, she closed her eyes and visualized another face, transposing the two in her mind. Within seconds, the two overlays clicked. Sherry exhaled sharply, opened her eyes, and did the math. If the CIA seemingly closed the project in 1994, that left seventeen years since the picture was taken. The man she stared at had a trademark look of confident power. Cadence McShane, an FBI agent training with the CIA remote viewing group. The two men were one and the same. But that conclusion forced the obvious question. What brought an FBI agent to a semi-arid desert in Texas? Particularly, to Grandfather's ranch?

The vast, West Texan plains had never been strategically important, and there wasn't a military base in the area. Further north, the once prolific oil fields were played out and the rest of the region survived with ranching and agriculture. The only city of any size, Amarillo, had often been referred to as a truck stop on the way to Los Angeles.

Sherry nibbled her thumbnail and came to an uncomfortable prospect. Pantex, located just minutes from east Amarillo, was the final assembly and disassembly point for all nuclear weapons in the U.S. Here, politically conservative, security-conscious workers tended to weapons of mass destruction. Logic dictated that any disruption or attack on the plant would have dire consequences on the surrounding states, and also create repercussions for the current administration.

Something crashed in the living room and she quickly closed the screen. Turning the PC off, she hurried down the hall in time to see the screen door slamming into the side of the house, buffeted by the wind.

"Is anyone there?"

Leaves from the elm tree rustled outside, and a shadow moved across the floor.

Lightfeather came into view and asked, "Did you call?" Catching the screen when it swung back, he nodded. "Are you ready?"

Sherry peered into the bedroom down the hall and gratefully stepped outside. She scanned the house as they got into the truck. It appeared empty, yet she couldn't shake her uneasiness.

Sherry took a deep breath to calm down. "Have you seen Cadence?"

"I think he's in the workshop."

"For sure?"

Lightfeather raised an eyebrow. "Everything okay?"

"Oh, yeah." Her gut said something different, though.

CADENCE'S FINGERS MOVED SWIFTLY ON the keyboard while he typed *"www.a"* into the PC's address box. The dropdown showed the previous addresses, none of which interested him. Moving through *www.b, www.c, www.d,* he impulsively jumped to *www.r,* and his intuition paid off. He uncovered the Google hit for remote viewing. Hammering a series of key strokes to uncover Sherry's last link, he found a declassified picture from seventeen years ago. Of all the damn bad luck. He'd physically changed since that image had been taken and no one should have made the connection, but the unexpected always happened and things could be taken care of. Tapping his finger against the keypad, he admitted, "Now, we have a problem."

MYSTIC PIZZA

SHERRY STOOD WITH LIGHTFEATHER ON the porch of a home in the working-class sector of Amarillo. A quiet neighborhood with quaint charm was an unusual place for a mystic to live. Yet stranger things had happened in the past few days.

"I want to prepare you for Mr. Irby, so don't be surprised." He knocked, and the door flew open to reveal a deliciously plump black woman with flashy gold, customized teeth.

"Lightfeather! Mr. Irby sayin' you come today." She gave him a sexy wink. "I make yo favorite pie, garden rhubarb. Come do it proud with a sip of milk."

Lightfeather stepped inside, and she wrapped herself around him, enveloping him in her glorious bosom and fleshy arms. She giggled and mahogany flesh rippled and danced with her laughter.

Lightfeather tried to hug back but was out of luck. She was too wide, and his arms weren't long enough, but that didn't stop him from trying.

She finally let go and her smile spoke volumes about Lightfeather. Stepping back, she untied her apron and threw it into the kitchen. "Mind you, we got manners here. I'm sure you be Sherry, and I be Momma Leitha."

Leitha took Lightfeather's wrist and yanked him toward the kitchen. "Mr. Irby down the hall, honey." She wiggled her plump hand in the opposite direction. "Locomote, sweetie, don't make him wait."

As the two disappeared from view, Lightfeather erupted with a gut-busting laugh and Leitha squealed with glee.

Sherry couldn't picture them together, yet their laughter emphasized something had been going on for awhile. Focusing on the reason for her visit, she took a deep breath and walked down the hall. The last doorway on the left was layered with multi-colored beads, and when she stepped inside, darkness hemorrhaged under a black light that bled waves of electric gloom. Psychedelic posters from the seventies adorned the walls, and an eight-track played a vintage Led Zeppelin song. Four lava lamps pulsed with orange blobs that morphed into human-like fetuses and a bundle of smoldering sage released a soothing aroma. Behind a metal desk, a tall swivel chair turned to reveal a tiny black male with untied sneakers on the wrong feet. His child-sized jeans were turned up with four-inch cuffs and a small T-shirt showed a clenched fist with *Black Panthers Live* in lightning-bolt script. Dwarfed by the chair, he wiggled his feet and smiled innocently. His snow-white afro contradicted his little boy body, but what captivated Sherry was the power of his gaze. His star-burst silver eyes revealed uncommon depth and tested her sense of emotional security. She felt like her secrets were revealed and incredibly, understood. The eyes were the pathway to the soul, and his bestowed a jolt of the unfathomable.

He pointed a marinara-stained finger toward a plate on the desk. "Pizza?"

"Looks good, but no thanks."

A smile chased the wrinkles on his tiny face as he watched Sherry.

Looking for something to break the intensity of the moment, she clasped her hands. "I'm...."

"Sherry," he answered for her. "And, of course, call me Mr. Irby."

She asked, "Did Lightfeather tell you why I'm here?"

He wolfed down a bite of pizza, wiping his lips on the back of his arm. "We visited." The little man finished chewing and cleared his throat. "Lightfeather told me of your psychic awakening, but my intuition speaks of another, more personal issue."

Sherry turned her eyes down.

He took a moment to bring his legs to his chest and wrapped his arms around them. "Those who come to my door are searching for answers. Sometimes we find insight in a simple discussion."

Mr. Irby pursed his lips and closed his eyes. His slender nostrils flared as he swayed from an inner beat. "In the critical moments of life, when we're presented with personal or spiritual dilemmas, we are often faced with several paths. God grants you free will to pick one, be it for better or worse. But know this, Sherry. There's always time to change the toad you're on."

She cocked her head and nearly smiled. His word choice was interesting as she substituted road for toad, yet, the rest of the message hit home. With brutal clarity, she remembered the monk's prophetic words. 'Before you laid a path of good and evil, life and death, and you chose wisely. But then you lost your way.'

Mr. Irby opened his eyes. "Do you think it applies? Have you been given a second chance to right the path?" He kicked off his worn sneakers, sipped from a frosted glass of milk, and arched an eyebrow. "There is tension within you and it is there to stay. Until you agree to tread the toad less traveled."

Sherry substituted the word road a second time and focused on what the message meant to her. Change sometimes appeared like a disturbance within the mind, giving the impression of discord. Yet, mental discomfort could facilitate choosing the correct path, and that decision would bring awareness and insight.

Mr. Irby dug in his pocket and removed an Oreo. Picking off the lint, he dunked it in the milk and popped it in his mouth. With a sense of satisfaction, he leaned back in his chair and chewed it quickly. Locking his hands behind his head, he took a breath. "The winds of change are upon you, and your feet ache for the path beneath them."

As Sherry reflected upon her choice, she knew the psychic path was hers to follow. A relationship beaconed from her awakening. It was true that she had used her ability to uncover Cadence's true identity, but was the psychic knowledge of her visions evil like her parents had always said?

Mr. Irby narrowed his eyes and smiled. "You've been shown a new direction, and I sense you'll answer in the spirit it was given. Even though things have changed, you are still the same unique person with individual strengths and weaknesses." He lifted his tiny hand. "The road less travelled is meant for you, but it will take exceptional courage on your part.

"Your past is a predictor for future success, because you've always tended the seed of discovery for better or for worse. Most times the bitter fruit of suffering brought you strength. And, though your failures emphasized your weakness, you've overcome them.

"On a different note, when your soul is consumed with mental illness, some laugh at your illogical words. But in the spirit of light and grace, you do not laugh at the verbal mistakes of others. Or the calculated butchery of my word choice."

Mr. Irby scooted out of his chair and stretched like a cat. "Now, I have something to show you. Something I made in kindergarten." He padded to the shadows and opened the lid of a battered toy chest. Removing a yellow Tonka truck and an old cigar, he finally grabbed a worn picture album. Blowing dust off its cover, he solemnly placed it in Sherry's lap.

The frayed cloth was rough against her fingertips when she opened the cover. The paper inside was faded and covered with brittle plastic, yet when she turned the page, a square mirror was glued in the middle. She stared at her reflection and arched an eyebrow.

Mr. Irby wrinkled his forehead and he lit the cigar. He took a deep puff and contemplated his words. "When I was searching for answers, I had my epip— epiphan.... Anyway, kindergarten was a good year. I learned a lot about life." A white cloud of smoke floated through the glare of the black light and vanished in the darkness above. "I know you have struggled with schizophrenia and need a perspective." He paused a moment and tapped ash off his cigar. His face wrinkled in concentration. "When in the grip of mental darkness, you bleed, but don't know why. You see the wound, yet you're blind to the cause." He gently patted Sherry's arm, and whispered, "Read the words below."

In red crayon, it read, *I FEAR THAT WHICH LIES WITHIN ME. I FEAR THAT WHICH I AM.*

Sherry cringed. Her heart missed a beat.

Mr. Irby steepled his fingers. "Look in the mirror, Sherry. Recognize the schizophrenia and psychic awareness within you."

With deliberate intent, she stared at her reflection.

He puffed again, and orange ember flared. Lying down on his sleeping mat, he gave a little sigh. "If you recognize it, its power is diminished. Say its name, and you control it." He smiled. "With time, truth shall set you free."

In silent rhythm, tears trickled down her cheeks and fell upon the page. She hung her head and whispered, "I fear that which I am."

THE THREE TUNNELS

THE RIDE TO HIGHLAND NURSING Home was made in deep silence. Sherry stared out the window and didn't move even when the truck stopped.

Lightfeather touched her arm. "Go visit Ben and Cindy."

"Oh, wow." Rubbing her eyes, she looked around. "I'm totally gone. Sorry."

"Mr. Irby has that effect on people. Digs through the armor and pulls your guts out."

"Yeah. He didn't make exceptions because I'm a woman, either." She mustered a faint smile. "He gets points for consistency, though." Still deep in thought, Sherry glanced over at the nursing home. "I'll see you in an hour. I need this break after Mr. Irby." Pausing for a moment, she looked up, "Okay if I stay at the ranch this weekend?"

"Never been a problem. Cadence won't mind, either."

Sherry hoped her wicked look would melt the scales off of Lightfeather. "So... what about you and Leitha?"

"What about us?"

"You were having way too much fun. You know, there in the kitchen."

"There are things about me you don't know. All you ever had to do was ask."

"I'm asking. Now."

"Too bad. You've gotta go visit and I've gotta go. Now." Lightfeather put the truck in drive and edged forward.

Sherry swatted him on the arm and opened her door. "Talk later?"

"Depends."

"We need a heart-to-heart. You know, open up. Access your feminine side."

Love shone in his dark eyes when he barked, "Will you get your butt out, or do I need to drag you inside?"

"I can take a hint." She jumped out and shouted, "Love ya," slamming the door before he could growl back. Sherry always got the last word in.

TWO MONTHS AGO, SHERRY HAD been on a medevac search and rescue at the Taos pass, outside of Angel Fire, New Mexico. The team had been searching for a pair of mentally challenged adults who had wandered off into the wilderness during a picnic in the forest. The couple, Ben and Cindy, were both fifty-five and born severely mentally handicapped. Their nursing home in Amarillo, Texas routinely spent a summer afternoon in the national forest as a treat for its mobile residents.

During the outing, the two had wandered off, becoming separated from the staff for over one hour. Once they were confirmed missing, a distress call was made to Amarillo and a helicopter crew immediately dispatched. A short while later, Sherry and the team began searching where the couple was last seen. After fruitless hours of observation, fuel was low and the pilot ready to quit. But Sherry, on impulse, pointed to a thick stand of pine trees. She addressed the pilot on her helmet intercom, "Fly past those trees and look for a clearing on the downward side of the mountain."

The pilot glanced at the fuel gauge, worry marring his face. "We have an hour and a half flying time, that's it. Even if we refuel in Taos, it'll be dark when we get back."

"I've got a gut feeling," Sherry said while the helicopter hovered over the mountain peak. "Just go forward another hundred yards."

The pilot complied, and Sherry strained her eyes for the clearing she had seen in her mind. From their vantage point one hundred yards above the mountain, there was nothing but thick forest. For fifteen minutes, they searched the rough terrain. The pilot tapped Sherry's helmet and ran a finger across his throat. "I've got to terminate."

Sherry pointed. "The clearing. Right there."

"Where? I don't see it."

She gestured to a small meadow below, surrounded by thick pines. "Take us lower."

And to everyone's surprise, Ben and Cindy were in the sandy clearing looking up at them.

It had been a momentous day. The errant couple was rescued, returned home, and Sherry had made the game winning call.

Now, she sat in Ben and Cindy's room and remembered the back story revealed by the facility's staff. It was the custom in Ben and Cindy's generation to be sent to a state-supported institution for the mentally challenged to live under the care of sometimes indifferent, and often bored, minimal wage employees. The two lived and grew up in adjacent wings at the Austin, Texas Beachwood Sanitarium, and formed a deep attachment for each other. From an early age they were inseparable, and their world consisted of being as close to each other as possible. When they turned twenty-one, their parents consummated the couple's devotion with a simple wedding ceremony. It didn't matter that neither Ben or Cindy recognized the union, it just meant they could be together all the time, and the state's idea of dictating separation among residents could go screw itself.

Years slowly passed, and Ben and Cindy's parents died of natural causes. However, the wills bequeathed a generous annuity that allowed them to live in a comfortable setting for the rest of their lives. The innovative nursing home they were moved to was proud of a staff-to-patient ratio that set the standard for the rest of the nation. Yet, the couple's care went beyond that with 24/7 assistance.

Ben and Cindy's evening aide walked over and Sherry lifted her head and smiled. Jill, a pleasant, elderly woman with rosy cheeks and grandmotherly charm had befriended Sherry, and often doted on the couple's well being.

Jill adjusted her knitted shawl and smiled up at Sherry. "They make the perfect pair."

Cindy, who preferred her sweets over more nutritious fare, was surprisingly thin, being graced with porcelain skin, fine bone structure, and beautiful red hair. All her waking hours, she sat propped up on her bed, scribbling on a pad of paper. Ben was tall and naturally muscled and could have been a professional athlete if nature had not given him the mind of an infant. With undying devotion, he always sat at the end of Cindy's bed, within touching distance of his life partner. The couple had never learned to speak, yet Ben's expressive eyes followed Cindy's every move and innocent devotion showed on his face.

Sherry had been visiting them at the nursing home for two months and loved the gentle ways of this quiet couple.

Jill adjusted her bifocals. "It's about time."

Together, Jill and Sherry witnessed the intriguing routine.

Cindy finished her scribbling and looked at Ben. She tapped her pen three times in the middle of the paper and held her hand up.

Ben lifted his head and sang a short tune while Sherry murmured the corresponding musical notes, "F, A, C, E."

Cindy carefully removed her scribbled paper, set it to the side, and started drawing again. But something about the position of the paper caught Sherry's eye. She moved to Cindy's bedside and picked the sheet up. Holding it lengthwise, she exclaimed, "I never noticed this before, but Cindy has drawn her name three times across the page."

She showed it to Jill, who tilted her head and peered closely.

Sherry said, "If you look, Cindy uses chaotic strokes for each letter and surrounds them with what looks like topographic lines."

Jill clicked her dentures. "How quaint. All this time, I thought she was just doodling."

"Stranger still," Sherry continued, "It's like water rushing toward the three D's in her name, giving the appearance of a wild river entering three tunnels."

Jill pulled her shawl closer and shook her head. "My my. You have such an imagination." The aide sighed and looked at her Timex. "It's about time for their dinner. I guess you're finished, now?"

Sherry nodded. "Take care. I'll see you next week."

"Sounds good," Jill acknowledged. She gave Sherry a pat and saw her off with a soft, "Bye-bye."

JILL QUIETLY CLOSED THE DOOR to the couple's room and locked it. She dropped her shawl on the mahogany dresser and stood straighter. Removing a camera phone from her starched uniform pocket, she took a picture of Cindy's paper, transmitting it by punching in a number she'd committed to memory over two months ago.

Sweat ran down her spine, and she cursed herself while the phone rang.

On the sixth ring, it connected.

"We should have seen it." Jill spat the words. "Coming from what's left of their brains, they've been giving us a message." Her hand trembled while she gripped the phone. "Have you seen the picture I sent you?"

"I've got it now. It's small, can you detail it?"

Jill swept her gray hair back from her forehead. "Cindy's been giving us a clue. With a little imagination, it could be a river flowing into three tunnels."

"I'm accessing it, wait a minute."

Jill took a sharp breath, and the hair on her neck rose. "Goddammit. I know where they were. I know the location."

"I've got it now. I see the tunnels."

She tumbled the words out. "It's the River of Three Tunnels. On the edge of the Taos Pass. In New Mexico, just outside of Angel Fire. I grew up there. The local Indians called it sacred ground. And it's the same place they were found by the search and rescue team."

"You made a good catch."

"Me?" Jill snorted. "Their friggin' visitor caught it. Sherry Whittington. My memory was jogged when she mentioned the appearance of three tunnels."

Silence spilled over the cell connection.

Jill looked at the wall running parallel to Cindy's bed. "Just a minute." She focused the camera phone and took another shot. Transmitting the picture, she said, "Enlarge it. Tell me what the hell you see."

In utter disbelief, Cadence said, *"It's been under our nose for two months."*

Jill nodded and stared at thousands of Cindy's messages, stacked in neat, orderly rows against the wall. "Yeah. With all the FBI's resources, the fuckin' medevac tech figured it out.

AIN'T LOVE GRAND

LIGHTFEATHER PULLED IN FRONT OF the ranch house and slapped the steering wheel. "Going inside?"

"Not yet," Sherry replied. "Think I'll fill the Beemer's nitrous tank."

Lightfeather groaned like his teeth were being jerked out. "If you need to talk," he wheezed, "You know where I am."

Lightfeather was two parts vinegar and one part mushy soft inside, but she would never let on. He enjoyed being cranky and Sherry loved him despite himself. He had a nurturing side and was the one who consoled her when her father left. He'd held her close each time she cried. In the months afterward, his incredible devotion lifted her from despair. During the early years of her schizophrenia, Sherry remembered her mother's denial and callous statement that she was faking her mental illness. In a fit of rage, Lightfeather got two inches from Sabra's face, stabbed his finger against her chest and called her a stupid bitch who couldn't tell shit from Shinola. He'd made his point and had won Sherry's heart forever.

She acknowledged his offer with a kind smile and graced him with a love few ever earned.

As she stepped onto the pebbled drive to the workshop, the evening breeze was cool against her skin. The sun was descending behind a bank of monumental white clouds, transitioning the sky into a pool of ethereal beauty. Waning rays diffused into glorious reds and magnificent golds, creating an aura she had only felt in the great cathedrals of Europe. At the crest of the clouds, a riot of orange, pink, and lavender spilled over in iridescent harmony, completing the heart of this sacred panorama. Sherry took a deep breath and humbled herself as God's majesty called forth the wonder and mystery of a Texas sunset.

After one last look, she turned toward the darkened workshop where a subtle movement caught her eye. She focused on a shadowy figure and froze in place. Cadence was naked from the waist up and had his back toward her. His hairless torso glistened with light perspiration, which shimmered upon his broad shoulders. He held an electric grinder, and the muscles of his arms flexed in hypnotic rhythm while he ground a shaft of steel. Deft strokes shot sparks across the darkened shop, spewing metallic fire in an arc that fell near a pile of rags.

He shaped the metal with eloquence and precision while Sherry studied him closely. His tight-fitting jeans emphasized a flawless waist and a deep tan gave him a devilish appeal.

She couldn't look away, couldn't tear her eyes from him, couldn't deny he was an erotic dream that moistened her religious taboos with forbidden possibility. The crumbling defenses of her Fundamentalist upbringing were violated in a surge of sexuality, fed by the spontaneity of the moment. Then it happened. He turned around.

He put the grinder on the bench and cocked his head.

She eyed the definition of his chest and her stomach fluttered. His long ebony hair was tied in a pony tail and his nipples were tiny points on a perfect body.

The tension in the air was palpable as he sauntered toward her.

He gave a slow, confident smile and she stepped backward. Cadence closed the distance to three feet. Two feet.

And then their bodies touched.

As Sherry put her hands up to push him away, she looked up into his eyes. Raw desire stared back and breached her defenses. The breath jolted from her lungs. In a moment of insight, she realized that her erotic fantasies were now a possibility.

MOTHER SONJA BROODED IN HER dark living room, sitting on the couch that had captured Sherry's heart-shaped charm. The pallid glow from a guttering candle fell across *The Complete Idiot's Guide to Wicca and Witchcraft*, which she held upside down and inches away from her failing eyes.

She gave a little squeak, and said, "Oh bitch. I'm gonna hurt you now." Closing the book, she groped for the Gold Medal Flour and opened the flap. Carefully pouring the powder in a crude circle on the carpet, she created a protective sphere for her summoning spell.

Her wrinkled hands shook as she placed the candle in the center of the Witches' Circle. She didn't have the proper incense, so she sprayed Glade Air Freshener to cleanse the sacred space. What the hell. It always worked in the bathroom. She placed Sherry's charm at the base of the candle, and began to chant.

> *Break apart the earthly soil,*
> *Here to trouble, here to toil.*
> *Time to shine, now cross the line.*
> *Devil be free, oh come to me,*
> *With Satan's fire, I free you from mire.*

The tiny flame grew and flickered, casting eerie shadows upon the walls. Mother Sonja squealed in dark satisfaction when Churchill lumbered into the room. His black patch stretched tautly across his sightless eye. He cocked his head and sniffed the air. Looking at the candle, he gave a slobbery grin and strutted into the circle.

THE KISS DESTROYED SHERRY'S RESISTANCE and drowned her in dark, violent passion. Her ears roared and his tongue slipped between her lips, tasting faintly of cinnamon and cloves.

He kissed her, and she submitted to a chemistry that was part fiber and part soul. Sherry wrapped her arms around his waist and met his tongue with hers.

His hands moved from her back, to her waist, and then up to caress her breasts. He gave a guttural moan, picked her up, and carried her inside the shop. Cadence shoved the tools off the bench, scattering them across the floor. A three-liter bottle of cola spun wildly across the metal top as he set her down.

He crushed his lips against hers. Sherry trembled when he hooked his thumbs beneath her white cotton top and jerked it over her head. The dangerous look in his eyes was surgical steel on her inhibitions—cutting restraint to ribbons and setting her heart pounding. When he grabbed the front of her bra and ripped it apart, she kissed him harder.

His chest heaved and he sucked in air, panting like a wild animal. He put his lips upon her breast and raked her hardened nipple, back and forth, across his front teeth. Sherry threw her head back and screamed, for he'd delivered her to the realm of fantasy—a place where inhibitions died and passion began.

She put her hands upon his chest, hoping to push him away, but ever so slightly, decreasing her pressure. Sherry lowered her hands to his rib cage and stroked his stomach. In a haze of passion, Sherry made eye contact as she unbuckled his belt.

MOTHER SONJA SAT IN THE circle and rubbed her tiny hands together. She cackled and sprayed the Glade again, but the aerosol hit the candle flame, creating a pressurized fireball that ballooned across the circle and singed Churchill's whiskers.

"Oh my," she croaked.

Her look of surprise turned into a glimmer of lethal intent. Groping for the charm, Mother placed it on the other side of the candle. With brutal calm, she squinted her eyes and focused on the barely visible flame. Steadying her shaking hands, she pressed the button and screamed, "Burn in hell, bitch." The flammable aerosol shot downward, scorching the carpet and blistering the charm with a red-hot kiss.

WITHIN THE WORKSHOP, A SPARK glimmered and caught fire in the rags. One foot away, a can of gasoline sat next to a hundred-gallon propane tank. Pressurized rubber hoses from two cutting torches crisscrossed the floor, just inches from the growing flame.

Cadence pulled Sherry's pants off and threw them on the floor. He ripped his jeans open and lifted her off the table. With her back against the bench, and her feet on the floor, he placed his penis between her upper thighs, nestling it against the crotch of her panties. With single-minded pleasure, he dry-stroked Sherry, creating an erotic thrill that took him to the edge of climax. Cadence threw his head back and thrust harder, slamming her against the bench, shaking the table and jarring the bottle of cola.

On the other side of the table, the pressurized hoses began to smoke, and the flames licked the edge of the gas can.

CHURCHILL SQUINTED HIS GOOD EYE and squared off with Mother Sonja. Drool ran down his chin and he snorted with disdain.

She lined the Glade up for a final shot, just as Churchill waddled to the candle. Lifting his hind leg, he peed directly on the flame, extinguishing it with a hiss just as Mother sprayed the Glade. The blast of deodorizer caught him on the flank, and he scampered off into the darkened room.

AS CADENCE THRUST AGAIN, THE action jarred the cola over the side of the bench. Hitting the concrete floor, the plastic neck cracked and sprayed liquid into the nearby fire. The bottle whipped around from the intense pressure, sending cola high into the air, covering Cadence and Sherry with sticky liquid.

AS THE COLA RAN DOWN their bodies, Cadence held Sherry tight. She gasped and looked up into his dark eyes. They were both covered with sweet, sticky liquid, and laughter bubbled up within her. Kissing his cheek, then the tip of his nose, she giggled. "Timing's everything, Bubba."

Cadence's body trembled and he pulled away slowly. After a minute, he caught his breath and brushed a drop of brown liquid off her chin. His eyes were unfocused. "Yeah, it is." He looked around and sniffed the air. "You smell somethin' burning?"

"I sure do."

They both scanned the workshop, looking for the source of smoke, until Cadence pointed behind them. "Probably a grinding spark in the rags." He bent over and retrieved his jeans and her clothes. "Changing the topic, I think we need to talk about things. No better place than a road trip. You in the mood?"

Sherry put her clothes back on, the ones that weren't ripped to shreds, and answered, "I'm off the day after tomorrow. What do you have in mind?"

"New Mexico."

She was taking a big chance, but Sherry had tempted the devil within and liked what she'd seen. "Count me in. But, I've got some questions for you."

"Thought you'd say that." He narrowed his eyes and gave a wicked grin. "Afterwards, we'll finish what we started here."

UNLEASH THE BEAST

EVIL STRIPPED THE BONDS OF its unholy lair and rose in the night. With unfettered power, it hissed and gurgled, and whispered words only Morda could hear. Lying upon his bed, he closed his eyes to receive its will, to worship that which destroyed its servants. The whisper was cruelly seductive, taunting him with silken promises of degradation and obscenity yet unborn. From those words, Morda's awareness prickled on the edge of epiphany as he sensed brute power and demonic hunger. Janette's ungodly rendition of *Ave Maria* had unleashed the Beast within him and he basked in the fold of true evil.

Another presence intruded upon this communion when Morda sensed the nearness of his musical servant. He breathed in and tasted the scent of her darkest secrets, her deepest fears. And, for the first time, he reached out to touch her, bestowing tribute to her twisted genius. Moving his arm slowly, he found her inches from his bed. Running his fingers across her supple flesh, he knew something was different and sensed her words before she knew them.

A shaft of moonlight broke through the room's window and fractured the embrace of darkness. In that faint light, Morda savored the milky softness of Janette's sightless eyes. He placed his hand around hers.

"It's late," she said.

"No," he stated, knowing her intent. "You cannot go." Her blindness and innocence aroused him, spooning him the rich pabulum of profound sadness.

He absorbed her vulnerability, gorging himself on her weakness. Vague memories of his own violation jolted his need for domination. While his past guided his future, the darkest part of his heart rebelled against the spark of goodness that still dwelt within him.

Janette stroked his stomach with a sensual touch.

"I have to go," she whispered.

Morda sighed deeply. "If you must, but you'll play when I return from New Mexico?"

She paused and her soft laughter pulsed in the night.

Morda fed upon the purity of her response and sucked the life from it until silence reigned again.

Yet, for all his demands, she slipped from his grasp and silently left the room.

When Morda stretched and beckoned the Beast within, Janette's gentle voice floated through the door. "For you, I'll always be there."

CROSSING THE LINE

THE SPEED OF CADENCE'S JEEP imparted a strobe effect from the broken light of the tree canopy above. While the warm patter of sunlight crossed Sherry's face, the fresh New Mexico mountain air invigorated her with the scent of cool, aromatic pine.

Cadence reached to place his hand in hers, and his eyes were as inviting as the gentle foreplay of light upon water. He had been quiet since they left Texas four hours ago and she was certain Cadence had discovered her remote viewing inquiry. She took pride in her knowledge. However, it came more from intuition than logical analysis. When the moment came to reveal his true identity, she would be in the dominant position, so she indulged his subtle seduction with a smile.

He glanced back at the road. "We'll stop in a mile, and hike to the location. I've got the gear we'll need an' afterwards we'll settle in Taos."

"That's," she wanted to say great, but her world morphed into black and white. Sherry was enveloped with a strange sensation that delivered her soul to the deserted Texas field where pumpkins lay in mounds upon the parched earth. Her hallucination hemorrhaged reality by delivering a scarecrow, dressed in shabby pants and a chambray shirt. A knife slashed downward, ripping the scarecrow's garment, sending bits of straw into the fall wind.

But this time, it was different. Her mental break always evoked fear, and she had no control over the images that spewed forth and overwhelmed her. Now, for the first time, she saw a child gripping the knife handle and recognized his blood-stained weapon as a cheap Halloween toy. Costumed children danced around him, screeching in delight while he stabbed the straw man.

Watching over the mock assault was the grizzled giant from Sherry's childhood, the Scarecrow Man. The gentle creature jumped up and down, clapped his hands, and urged the boy to assault his creation.

A gust of wind spawned dust devils, and the dry Texas wind whipped the children's costumes around their bodies, flapping against thin legs and arms. Soon tiring of the mock assault, they ran across the street to the Halloween Carnival. With his audience gone, Scarecrow Man hung his head and mumbled, "It's Halloweenie." Jerking into motion, he shambled after the children and crossed the road without looking either way.

Young Sherry was standing in the middle of the pumpkins, and a hand encircled hers. She looked up at her mother, who smiled as she said, "Love you, sweetie."

The hallucination dissipated, and for the first time since Sherry was twelve, the veil of fear had parted. Somewhere inside, she glimpsed a deeper message, for it had the feel of substance and memory.

Cadence banked the truck into a sharp turn and bumped over stone and dirt ruts until they came to a stop. He stomped the emergency brake and a thin layer of dust washed over them.

"You okay?" he asked.

Sherry had crossed a line by allowing him into her world. For a moment, she was back with Mr. Irby, looking into his mirror. She didn't know where to start, so she took a deep breath. "I've had the same hallucination since I was twelve. But this time, something's different."

"Better or worse?"

"Better, I think. Like the missing piece of a puzzle."

His brow furrowed. "What's it like? Your schizophrenia?"

"You want the truth?" Sherry looked him in the eye.

"If it doesn't bother you."

There were personal issues she needed to face, and now was as good a time as any to address them. "Because of my schizophrenia, I keep a tight grip on reality. When you don't have control over your mind, you constantly fear losing it. Consequently, you obsess over your environment. If you see something out of the corner of your eye, you have to glance back and see if it's real. You're always watching people's body language or listening closely to what they say. God help you if they're ambiguous or illogical because you don't have the calm reasoning to realize they just made a mistake. The fear within distorts your perceptions and eliminates the finer aspect of understanding your environment. It's a vicious cycle of your perceptions triggering your fear and your fear affecting your perceptions." She paused. "I keep such a tight grip on reality, that if it was a man, I'd have choked him to death.

"But step up the fear with my life-long hallucination. Before it occurs, it's like the beginning of Alice in Wonderland. Everything's fine. But when the images come, thoughts that were once calm and logical are destroyed with hellish intensity, setting the platform for a nightmare. It feels like you've had twelve cups of coffee, and you're wired. Your mind screams with razor intensity. Then, it's Alice on Acid, and reality gets a foot in the face."

Sherry looked out at the forest. The cooling engine popped while the surrounding pines rustled. In the distance, a crow cawed. The afternoon sun baked their truck.

"Is it that bad?"

She gripped his hand and looked into his eyes. "Yeah, it's that bad." She scanned his face and detected a mischievous look.

He traced his finger against the back of her hand. "Can't be worse than a stick in the eye?"

His timing was impeccable. Sherry grimaced. "I'd rather eat worms."

"Couldn't be worse than liver."

She shook her head and rolled her eyes. "Nothing's worse than liver."

"You know, just being around you, I'd never suspect what went on inside that brain of yours. Sometimes things aren't what they appear to be."

He removed his hand from hers and his eyes had a distant quality. "Cadence McShane isn't who he appears to be, either." He delivered his words in a flat, Midwestern accent. "And we both know it."

A VANISHING RIVER OF SAND

DAMN CADENCE—OR WHOEVER THE hell he was. After he had delivered his statement, he put his pack on and walked away from the truck. Sherry struggled to keep up while they trekked through the dense forest, along a path that hadn't seen footprints in years. She lost sight of him for the third time, and angrily stomped over decades of fallen pine needles. The vague trail broke left, then angled sharply upward. The high altitude had her panting when she entered a small opening set above a broad valley. He stood near an unlocked fence covered with razor wire and pointed to a sign above.

Sacred Tribal Land. No Trespassing.

She didn't want to know how he got the key.

He pulled a cigarette from behind his ear and loosened his ponytail. Shaking out a lustrous mane of ebony hair, he flinted up with a Zippo and took a deep drag. She never knew he smoked. Add another ounce of issue to the pound of questions for Mystery Man.

He gave a curt nod. "Follow me."

They stepped through the open gate, walked to the edge of the cliff, and peered at the valley below. An ancient stairway carved into the face of native granite dropped sharply for a hundred feet before reaching the bottom. Sherry faltered and was reminded of her abortive attempt at skydiving last summer. She placed her hand on Cadence's shoulder to steady herself.

"Are you okay?"

She grinned sheepishly. "I don't do heights well."

Cadence smirked. "You're a medevac tech who's afraid of heights?"

"As long as I'm standing on something solid, I'm okay."

Cadence looked away and surveyed the valley below. Raising his hand to shade his eyes, he stared with gritty intensity. After a moment, he said, "You know who I am. That I was involved in a joint CIA/FBI remote viewing project. So don't bother me with questions about my past."

"Then why am I here?" Sherry's voice was sharp.

He hesitated a moment before spreading his hands. "I need your abilities. Someone who psychically picked up my connection with the FBI is incredibly perceptive. I also heard the story about how you followed your gut and rescued Ben and Cindy. Intuitively, I knew you were gifted before you read me." He motioned with a sweep of his hand. "This land holds a key—one that can prevent a tragedy—and I need your help."

Cadence flicked the ember from his cigarette and put the butt in his jeans pocket. "How did you discover my connection with the CIA remote viewing?"

"When I held your hand at the ranch, I was bombarded with images. I saw you briefing your men for a remote viewing exercise and I wanted to see if it was true. So, I googled remote viewing and found you."

"You accessed a minor chakra," he stated. "I assume you know what the briefing was about."

"This is a national security issue?"

Cadence broke eye contact and scanned the valley below. "Tell me what you see," he asked in a conciliatory tone.

"A valley bordered by mountains with a stream on the edge."

"See any tunnels?"

Sherry concentrated on the land and thought hard. The cool mountain breeze stirred her hair, and momentarily, she remembered. Biting her bottom lip, a response popped into her mind. "There are thousands of pages where Cindy scribbled her name. From what I saw, it looked like a river rushing into three tunnels."

Then it dawned on her. "You're looking for the River of Three Tunnels."

Respect showed on his face. "Exactly. So, where are the tunnels?"

She looked down, beyond the worn steps, and examined the forest again. It extended for a quarter mile, and when she scanned the area closest to them, she observed a large rectangle of bare land covered in sand.

She tapped her chin and focused on the trees, keeping the sandy rectangle in her peripheral vision. Squinting for a moment, she almost missed it. Until her thoughts clarified. "You're looking for a physical river leading into three tunnels."

Cadence nodded at the obvious.

He was making nice, but she was still pissed about his lies. "Try and think outside the box for a change," she goaded. "Who says tunnels have to start like a mining shaft in the side of a mountain?"

"What are you getting at?"

She picked up a cane-sized stick and pointed to the sand below. "Look closer, and you'll see the faint outline of three entrances—below the ground. You were searching for the obvious. Cindy's drawing wasn't showing a river of water. It's a river of sand you're looking for."

He stared at the faint contours and his face reddened. "I'll be damned."

Without further comment, Sherry headed for the steps and tried not to look down. When she reached the bottom, she was winded and her hiking boots sunk into the soft sand. "We've found the tunnels, so how do we get inside?"

The crunch of his footsteps coming from behind suddenly triggered her anger, and the full weight of his deceit overwhelmed her. Sherry was going to drop the proverbial shit in the fan and he didn't even know it. "It's time we had this talk," she snapped. "Everything about you is a lie. Who you are and why you've been working at the ranch is a good start. Furthermore, Ben and Cindy were never mentally challenged, and I'll bet they never grew up in a sanatorium."

Cadence turned his palms up, and she raised her voice. "They were working for you and found the tunnels. Then something happened to them. Something really bad."

He lowered his head. "True. Their last communication was over two months ago, when they reported a lead in the Taos Pass. After that, they dropped off the radar. Your med evac team found them right here." He paused and motioned with his hand at the plot of sand. "The truth is, Sherry, whatever's down there fried their brains." Cadence scuffed the sand with his hiking boot and crossed his arms. "So, we created a history for Ben and Cindy, filling in back story to throw you and the rescue team off. We put them in the nursing home, hoping to gather clues.

"It's true that I lied to you and your grandfather but lying is a part of my job. You don't live long in this business by telling the truth." Cadence spread his arms. "The real reason I came to work at the ranch was because our remote viewing showed us the object we're looking for is somewhere on your Grandfather's land." He nodded for emphasis. "But it's hard to find a small object in twenty square miles of prairie."

Cadence paused and shaded his eyes from the sun. "We also intercepted a message to a psychopath the bad guys are employing—a hermaphrodite named Morda. It seems that Morda will receive a shit load of money when she obtains the same ancient crystal we're looking for. A weapon with devastating powers."

He stepped close to Sherry and put his finger under her chin. "What happened between us at the ranch was real, and I never lied about that."

Sherry wasn't ready to let him off the hook, so she thumped his chest with her finger. "Cindy's drawing held the key, and you didn't even know it."

Cadence shaded his eyes from the midday sun. "That's beside the point, Sherry. We've got to get inside, and don't have time to place blame."

The sting of truth lanced her anger. "Cindy got us this far," she said in a softer tone, "and my gut says we're missing something. Have you watched her drawing in the nursing home?"

Cadence swept his ebony hair back. "What are you getting at?"

She closed her eyes and saw Cindy on the bed, scribbling her name across the paper. Each letter flowed into the next until she finished. When it was done, she poised her pen above the middle D in her name and tapped three times. Sherry opened her eyes and smiled. "It can't be that simple."

"What?" Cadence leaned toward her.

Gripping her walking stick, she raised it high. "Watch and learn." She stood above the top center of the tunnel, represented by the middle D in Cindy's drawing, and slammed the butt of the stick into the ground three times.

Seconds ticked by and nothing happened. Overhead, small clouds drifted across the sun and water gurgled down the stream. Cadence looked at her expectantly, so she slammed the stick again, three more times, into the sand-covered earth.

Cadence exhaled harshly. "I'll airlift an excavator and in twelve hours we'll start digging."

Sherry got a better grip on the stick, ready to slam the sand again, when a vibration rose up her feet. "Do you feel something?"

"What?"

"That faint tremor."

A trembling from below transmitted through the sand, and she shuddered. An image of ancient machinery deep in the earth, meshing gears and engaging cogs, gripped her imagination. Sherry whispered, "This is not good."

Cadence jerked around, his face twisted with fear. He stood in the middle of the entrance and sand began draining downwards, creating a vortex that engulfed his feet. He turned to run, but the surface collapsed, pulling him into the receding mass.

His torso disappeared, and his neck and face went under. Sherry watched his clenched fist vanish in the retreating sand.

Cadence was gone.

Tons of sand had drained in a violent flow, leaving a circular, sloping surface. Sherry scrambled to get to the top of the tunnel entrance but started to slide on the inclined circle. Her boot caught a tentative grip, and she pushed against the foothold, desperate to reach safety. She lunged for the stone rim but was inches short of the edge. Sherry slammed into the surface and the breath hammered from her lungs.

She dug her fingernails into the surface, pressed her boots against the side, trying to stop her downward motion, but the dark opening was just feet away.

Sherry looked up at the sky and glimpsed sunlight breaking through the clouds. She was bathed in soft, white light, and everything slowed. The seconds were like minutes, and she realized she was caught between the opposing force of life and death. Yet the subtle hue of spirituality spread within, and she realized that fear could not exist in this plane. The presence of God surrounded her, and she thought of those she loved. In the span of a wing beat, Sherry made her peace.

She plunged through the tunnel's eye, fell through the darkness below. The wind whipped across her body and she thought of Lightfeather.

I love you.

ON THE CLIFF OVERLOOKING THE valley, Morda had watched Cadence disappear and Sherry sliding down after him. After a little pause, she whispered, "How interesting," then padded down the steps to the opening below.

DARKNESS WITHIN

SHERRY HURTLED DOWNWARD AND THE sunlit opening got smaller. Harsh wind rasped across her body. Even though it was dark inside, she sensed immense space around her.

Cadence was already dead, or gravely injured, and Sherry would be next. She closed her eyes and seconds later, her shoulders smashed into something solid, and the air bludgeoned from her lungs. Her head snapped back and her muscles wrenched. Pain knifed through her body.

Yet strangely, the undiscerning reaper called Death didn't claim her life. She tumbled, side over side, head over heels, and plummeted downward, on the outer edge of a great sand hill. She wrapped her arms around her chest and scissored her legs. The sand that trapped Cadence and previous visitors was also a buffer against a deadly fall, letting her roll down its sloping edge in a controlled descent until she tumbled to the bottom.

In the semi-darkness, she squirmed on the stone floor and gripped her legs to her chest. Her lungs were on fire and she couldn't breathe. Hoping nothing was broken, she struggled for air just as Cadence's hands eased under her back.

Thank God he was alive.

"Relax." Cadence lifted her up. "The air will come."

Stars popped before her eyes and, mercifully, she finally inhaled. The musty cavern air filled her lungs with the sweetest, most intense breath she'd ever taken.

He gently ran his hands over her back, arms, and legs. "Nothing's broken, but you'll be sore tomorrow."

"You moron," Sherry gasped, "I'm sore as hell now."

"Humor's good. You're gonna live."

As she gulped air, Cadence shifted and removed an odd-looking gun from his backpack.

"What's that?"

"Watch and learn." He pulled the trigger and a flare shot upward, moving in a graceful arc.

When it reached the edge of its trajectory, it stopped and began floating downward, casting a bright, magnesium aura inside the cavern. Sherry realized they were at the bottom of an immense sand pile that had saved their lives. From the size of it, they weren't the first to drop in. Adding another mystery to the situation, the cavern walls began to glow with the soft blush of eggshell blue.

"This ain't the happy hotel," Cadence dead panned. "But somebody just turned the light on for us."

She unwrapped her arms and finally breathed normally. "Why's it glowing?"

"Don't know. Never seen anything like it."

They stood on the edge of an enormous cavern—it was shaped like a stadium dome, probably three hundred yards deep and a hundred across. From where she sat, it didn't look like nature made it. The dome was smooth, symmetrically balanced, curving gracefully from top to bottom, which meant solid rock was sculpted by someone with serious technology. Sherry absorbed the immense presence of the cavern, awed by its majestic power.

The flare settled on the ground, waned to a soft hue, and faded away. By the light of the dome's eerie glow, she saw a small moat surrounding a stone pedestal. A crystal sphere the size of a bowling ball sat on top and began rolling in place. Flashes of brilliant, rainbow colors pulsed from the base and impacted the ball's upper surface, only to fragment into thousands of multicolored sparks. The light surged every other second, giving rise to the similarity of a beating heart.

Cadence's eyes widened. "Damn."

Sherry already knew. This was what he'd hoped to find.

He stood and took a step toward her. "Here, let me help you."

She staggered to her feet and exhaled from the shock. "I can make it." But, her body was in serious denial.

He offered his arm and she stumbled to the edge of the moat. Ten feet of translucent, milk-colored water surrounded the pedestal and kept them from the spinning orb.

Cadence removed his boots and socks and stepped to the edge of the liquid. "Here goes."

Sherry gripped his arm. "Not a good idea."

"A little water never hurt anyone."

"Cadence, something here affected Ben and Cindy, and we need to think this through." She swept her hand and motioned to the sand behind them. "They came down the same way we did. If the cavern air didn't fry their brains, it had to be the water."

Cadence crossed his arms. "Go on."

"We've been here, what, ten minutes? So we rule out the air." She pointed to the liquid. "It's got to be the water. If so, you're too sexy to spend the rest of your life as a vegetable."

"What are you getting at?"

A thought trickled from the back of her mind. "Cindy's message showed us how to enter the tunnel, and I'm sure Ben's tune is another clue."

Cadence put his hands on his hips. "Okay, Cindy gave us one answer. So, what do the notes mean?"

A muscle cramped in her back and she leaned to the side to lessen the strain. "I was in high school choir, and Ben's four notes were F A C E."

Cadence gave the moat a sharp glance and stepped back. "Assuming they crossed the water, it got on their face, in their eyes, ears, and mouth."

"Yeah," she answered. "Whoever built this cavern wasn't making it easy to get to the orb."

Cadence stroked his chin. "Some biological agents can destroy the brain. If there are microbes in the moat, they're probably self-regenerating and have lived for God knows how long. Whoever built this place put the 'bug' in the water to protect the crystal sphere."

He tapped his foot, and for the second time that day, he looked at her with newfound respect. "Ben was warning us."

"Right on, Bubba. Now what?"

"The Boy Scouts say, 'Be Prepared.'"

He reached into his knapsack and removed a slender, black cylinder with a grappling hook on the end. Spooling out the steel cable, he swung the claw like a lariat, and whipped it across the moat and toward the base of the pedestal.

The claw wrapped around and overlapped the cable. With a tug, he cinched it securely.

"Ever roped cattle before?" she asked.

"If you're through talking," he answered with mock gruffness, "you can help me now."

Sherry followed him to the edge of the sloping, cavern wall where he bent and placed his hands upon the granite.

"Climb up my back and place the silver end of the metal tube against the stone. Reach up as high as you can and press the button on the side."

With a little jump, Sherry scampered upward, placed the cylinder against the wall, and mashed the button. A small explosion drove a steel anchor pin into the granite about nine feet above the floor. Without hesitation, she jumped down, interlocked her hands for his foot, and gave him a boost up.

Cadence gripped the tube, zip-lined down the wire, landed on his feet, and circled the spinning orb.

Suddenly, the pulsing light changed to crimson. Instead of shooting upward and shattering into a thousand sparks, it rebounded against the inner surface with the order of mathematical symmetry. Sherry watched it chart a geometric course, bouncing at equidistant points until a vivid, red triangle formed within. Ever so slowly, the triangle lost its brilliance and morphed into a revolving, miniature fireball.

She exhaled harshly. "What's going on?"

Before he could answer, a click signaled an internal change, and the orb stopped rolling. Hundreds of tiny holes appeared in the sphere's outer surface and the three-dimensional sun inside spun faster, throwing shafts of solar brilliance through the openings. Laser pinpoints escaped and speckled the giant ceiling above, appearing with distinct regularity, yet lacking form or purpose. When the light grew stronger, a definite pattern emerged. Each point grew in luminescence and size until hundreds of brilliant squares connected to form a huge screen across the ceiling.

Cadence's mouth dropped open. "Holy shit."

An immense island nation, seen from miles above, shimmered into focus. Scattered across the rich landscape was a vast network of roads connecting the metropolitan areas in the north with the agricultural areas in the south.

Momentarily, the left half of the screen zoomed to a close up of a large city, complete with tall, angular buildings and white-robed citizens.

Amid the bustling streets, people were surrounded with individual, white auras. While the serenity on their faces stirred her heart, she also sensed their profound, spiritual state.

As Sherry absorbed their presence with awe and humility, she was gripped by a dark insight. There was balance in all of nature, and mankind was no different. Since man's creation, good and evil have affected societies for better or for worse. Any civilization attaining great spiritual development has had an oppositional force of darkness. Evil was a catalyst which propelled good to grow and prosper. In a sense, the depth of a nation's depravity could fuel the height of its spirituality.

When the right half of the screen flickered, she feared her insight would bear fruit.

Lush crops were revealed, tended by young male laborers who all moved with the same precise motions. Each face was eerily similar, and the eyes, empty and blank. The men's homogenous appearance was unnatural and caused her spine to tingle. Hovering on the edge of discovery, Sherry squinted and focused on the workers' heads, trying to catch a trace of color. Then, it hit her in the gut. The workers did not have an aura. They lacked the gift that made us one with God, for they had no soul.

Somehow, the dark side of this ancient civilization genetically engineered a captive workforce, human in most respects, yet lacking a soul. This spiritual abomination offended her deeply, for it screamed that God was mocked in favor of material gain and a life of ease.

The enslavement of these 'things' was the disturbing chasm between the ethical north and the immoral south.

When the visual segments on the ceiling faded, an ancient power generator appeared, with large rectangular panels reflecting intensified sunlight into a small metal base holding a thin, three-foot crystal. Somehow, the six-sided mineral added a synergistic effect to the sun's energy, as it transmitted a stream of laser-like power toward an input receptacle. Oddly enough, there was a second crystal there, on the narrow stretch of bare earth at the base of the generator. It glowed ambient yellow and had a distinctive etching on its side, with a human eye centered inside a pyramid.

After the scene faded away, a flash of unimaginable power streaked across the cavern screen. Destruction raged against the cities and Sherry stifled a scream. The creators of the 'things' had turned their weapons against the benevolent citizens of the north. Chaos reigned, and the innocent were slaughtered with impunity.

The crystal's offensive power incinerated cities, buildings, and homes. Ultimately, the island nation was destroyed by earthquakes.

Cadence was stunned. "Is this land what I think it is?"

She was frozen in place and uttered one word. "Atlantis?"

The screen went dark and an image emerged, showing a crystal skull at the feet of the Egyptian Sphinx. Finally, a small box lay next to a hole in a barren stretch of dirt.

Sherry took a deep breath, and the sun in the revolving orb dimmed to a dying spark. The ceiling image faded to a pinpoint and then disappeared. Momentarily, the granite dome regained its soft, blue glow.

She glanced at Cadence as he bent down behind the pedestal. When he straightened, his face brightened with discovery. Donning a pair of thick gloves, he crossed the wire, hand over hand, dropping to the ground beside her.

"Sherry, I know...."

Before he finished, something whistled behind her, like the noise a club makes when it's swung hard. A black metal bat smashed across the back of Cadence's head, his eyes bugged out, and he hit the ground.

Stepping from the shadows, a tall, blonde woman in Spandex stalked toward Sherry.

"Who are you?"

"Morda."

With lightning reflexes, Morda jammed a black object against Sherry's stomach. There was the unmistakable crackle of electricity and a blast of high voltage knocked Sherry to her knees. Morda ran her tongue up her victim's neck and whispered, "Bitch, the party's just starting."

YOUR GREATEST
FEAR

WHEN SHERRY CAME TO, NAUSEA ripped through her body and she spewed a mixture of bile and blood. There, on the cavern floor amidst the yellow and red, was a piece of pink flesh. Her flesh. As she gingerly tongued the hole inside of her mouth, she realized she must have bitten her inner cheek after she passed out. Sherry tried to sit up, but her muscles trembled and her arms refused to work. After a moment, she faltered and plunged downward, into her vomit. The smell was ghastly, and she heaved what was left of her ham and cheese sandwich. She squirmed in the mess until it dawned on her to look down. Both her hands and feet were taped together. She moved sideways, struggled to a sitting position, and took a deep breath.

In a rush, she remembered Cadence being clubbed, and then her electric shock. Frantic to find him, she looked to her left, where he lay on the floor.

That disgusting bitch stood next to him with one hand on her hip and a bored look on her face. The corners of her lips turned up in a thin, cruel smile.

"Who the hell are you?" Sherry screamed.

"You should listen better. It's Morda."

In her skintight black Spandex, Morda's presence was disturbing. She was tall and lithe, with pubescent breasts and hips. A halo of blond hair framed her face, and she flipped it back so Sherry could see her clearly. Morda's arrogance bled from a source as dark as hell, and Sherry suddenly turned cold.

Momentarily, a moan escaped Cadence's mouth and his eyes fluttered. Morda squatted to remove a small rubber hose and one syringe from a pack on the ground. She wrapped the tourniquet around Cadence's upper arm and expelled the air from the hypodermic. After a deft thrust, she emptied the contents into his vein.

Fear cramped Sherry's stomach when she realized how vulnerable Cadence was. The man might die and there was nothing she could do to help him.

As Morda leaned back on her haunches, Sherry noticed her green reptilian eyes glittered with madness. Morda flipped her blond hair back. "If you had to be a candy bar, what would you be?"

Sherry was at a loss for words.

"No answer? I'll help you then. In your white bread world, you're plain cocoa and sugar. But in mine, I was born chocolate with extra fucking nuts. God made me this way."

Cadence began to stir.

Sherry struggled against her bonds and tape cut into her flesh.

Animal cunning tightened the corners of Morda's eyes. "I have a tidbit to share. Did you know that after the Bible, the most intriguing source of all knowledge is the National Enquirer? Their pundits said that fear of public speaking outranks the fear of dying."

Morda took a tube of hot pink lip gloss out of her pack and applied it carefully. "Does Cadence fear anything?"

Sherry shuddered.

Morda tilted her head. "Fear of public speaking is nothing compared to what I've done to him."

Morda helped Cadence sit up.

His face was expressionless, and a thin stream of drool ran over his bottom lip, onto his pants. But when he saw Sherry's face, his eyes glimmered with recognition.

Morda stared at her long nails and inspected their flawless color.

"What have you done?" Sherry screamed.

"I injected him with a permanent, mind-altering drug. He's still woozy from the blow I gave him. But in a few hours, he'll be nearly catatonic. He'll shit and piss himself like a baby. He won't talk anymore, but, I promise you, he'll be aware of everything."

Hot, searing pain sliced Sherry's heart.

Morda sighed and fluttered her hand. "Too bad. So sad." Her face brightened. "Are we having fun yet? You see, in our intimate gathering, Cadence is a little something to whet my appetite. And you, my dear, are next on the menu."

Morda brushed a nonexistent hair off her shoulder and laughed with a low, cruel sound. "My employer has a source in the FBI who told us about Cadence and his project here. You see, I represent certain people who desperately need the last crystal. It seems they want to wreak chaos on Washington, D.C.

"But I digress. The next point of business is the profile I got on you and your family. When I read it, I wondered, who deserved my immediate attention?" She tapped her long, thin finger against her cheek and pondered. "From what I learned, I'd do you a favor to eliminate your mother. And then, there's your father. But no one's seen him since that last tent revival. So, it all comes back to you. What's your greatest fear, Sherry?

"If memory serves me, your mental break was in your early teens. After several decades of sanity, can you imagine losing your mind again? Think of the horror you'll feel when it slips away, knowing your medication's out of reach. When I'm finished here, you'll sit in the dark and sense the burn in your brain." Morda give a mock salute. "I hope you enjoy the process as your mind implodes and psychosis begins."

Sherry's blood ran cold at the thought.

Morda strutted to the edge of the sand and looked up at the knotted rope she had climbed down on. "But losing your mind's not your greatest fear. Oh no, it's just an added topping. What I propose for you is so personal, so intimate, it will destroy you completely."

Morda put one booted foot on the sand and leaned toward Sherry. "Who's so close to you, you'd die to protect him? Who's been your closest friend and confidant? In my little banquet, Cadence was the aperitif, you're the entrée...."

Morda licked the tip of her finger and shivered with excitement. "And Lightfeather will be the fucking dessert."

Devastating pain welled from the bottom of Sherry's soul and ripped through her heart. Her scream echoed off the cavern walls. She struggled against her bonds and pleaded with God. Why me, why Lightfeather? What has Cadence done to deserve this? Finally, Sherry looked up in utter disbelief.

Morda slowly winked at her. "Just before I kill him, sweetie, I'll tell him you're dead."

THE THORAZINE
SHUFFLE

SHERRY'S CHEST HEAVED WITH A sob when she heard the sound of
hidden machinery coming into action. High above, the cavern opening was
closing. Morda was gone, and Sherry had no memory since Morda threatened
Lightfeather. This mental blackout was triggered by stress and randomly sucked
her awareness of prior events. One moment she was interacting with others and
the next moment everyone was gone. When this happened, she struggled with
the incomprehensible and didn't have a goddamn clue what just occurred. It was
a combination of bad mojo and mental illness that spawned this bastard of a
coping mechanism. So on a scale of one-to-oh, shit, this was *definitely* oh, shit.

Panic twisted Sherry's mind and it rendered her helpless. She had taken her
last dose of psychotropic medication five hours ago and was way overdue. Fear
lacerated her thinking and she instinctively brought her legs up to her chest.
In a fetal position, she rocked back and forth and drifted through a tapestry
of comforting memories. Sherry hummed a lullaby her mother used to sing to
her. From a distance, she heard laughter and the voices from her childhood. In
the protective embrace of her emotional cocoon, she remembered Mother and
Father waiting at the bottom of the slide for her.

"Come on down, honey," Daddy coaxed. "First time's the hardest, but
you'll be okay." He gave Sherry a half-smile and took Mommy's hand.

Young Sherry sat at the top of a very high, very scary slide, with her hands locked around the platform rail. Her bare legs rested on the top of the metal incline and she didn't want to let go. She gazed out over the park and her heart thudded in her chest. Large elm trees moved from the breeze and the sun warmed her face. Someone she knew was standing next to a stone wall, close to the baseball diamond.

Sherry looked back at Mommy, who leaned forward, put her hands around her mouth, and shouted, "Come down now. We haven't got all day."

Sherry needed to do something but wasn't ready.

Daddy hollered, "You heard your Mother. For Christ's sake, let go."

She scooted further onto the slide. Daddy looked at the ground and said the 's' word. He shook his head before he and Mommy walked away.

Wind blew Sherry's hair and the bright sun hurt her eyes. She wiggled even further down the sloping metal until her fingertips barely gripped the rail. From the edge of the park, Mommy slammed the car door and Daddy started the engine.

Sherry screamed, "Don't leave me," but the engine roared and Daddy shouted out the window, "You know the way home."

She closed her eyes and let go. The hot metal burned her legs as she slid faster and faster toward the hard, rocky ground. Sherry feared the gravel below, but when she shot out the end of the slide, rough hands caught her. Lightfeather lifted her to his chest and the warm smell of oil and gasoline filled her nose. Sherry snuggled her face into his neck. With tears in her eyes, she hugged him hard. "I love you."

As the memory of the slide faded away, Sherry returned to reality. Cadence was no longer drooling on his pants and rasped, "What the hell hit me?"

When she explained that Morda injected him with a drug that would make him catatonic in a few hours, Cadence's eyes opened wide and he looked away. He finally shook his head. "We need to concentrate on getting out of here, Sherry. I heard what Morda said about Lightfeather. We've got to help him before it's too late."

She agreed. The life of the man who had loved her more than anyone else now rested in her hands. Lightfeather had always been there when her parents ignored her, or worse, walked away. That strong, gentle man gave her his heart and taught her life's lessons with a firmness and love that took her breath away. He was her rock and she would die if she couldn't save him.

The time had come to do something and now she was ready.

With a plan in mind, Sherry gritted her teeth and banished the anxiety. She yelled at Cadence, "We're gettin' the hell out of Dodge, Bubba."

SHERRY USED HER TEETH TO rip the tape from her wrists, and then unwrapped her ankles. Cadence was still woozy from his head injury, but semi-conscious. It was Sherry's fervent hope to find a way out of this shit hole. "We need to start moving, Cadence."

Sweat ran down her face and they slowly walked across the cavern, stopping at times to allow Cadence to rest. The temperature was getting hotter and the walls bluish light faded. Lightfeather's fate was slipping away so she urged Cadence on. "We've got a ticking clock here." From deep inside, Sherry tapped an inner source of strength and dragged Cadence behind her. Her pulse pounded in her temple and she gasped her way across the granite floor.

Sherry slowed her pace, and he stumbled up behind her. "Can you walk any faster, Cadence?"

As they continued to move, an odd memory surfaced from Sherry's first psychiatric hospitalization. The heavy-duty mental patients back then all walked with the same thorazine- shuffle. They were stoned out of their minds and in a world of their own, but drugs had come far since the days of thorazine. If Cadence's situation wasn't serious, she might even laugh.

Sherry guided him across the cavern and prayed they were going in the right direction.

Fifteen minutes later, frustration had ground her anxiety to a fine point when they crossed the middle of the cavern. As if their situation wasn't bad enough, God thumbed his nose at them when the bluish light dimmed again. She could only see a few feet ahead of her, and had totally had it with Cadence. "Put your ass in gear," she shrieked. On impulse, she glanced into his eyes and realized he was doing the best he could. Cadence was all that held her from reaching Lightfeather and she silently raged against him. In the same beat, Sherry remembered the hunger of his hands on her body and his fervent kisses in the workshop. Guilt twisted her mind because she was torn between the two men in her life. Cadence, who lit her fire, and Lightfeather, who warmed her soul.

She focused on her watch and could barely see the dial, but thankfully they had reached the end of the cavern. The moment she had dreaded as they had made their way towards the end, happened. The bluish glow that had lit the cavern flickered and faded to total darkness.

Sherry fisted her hands and took several deep breaths. She gripped Cadence's upper arm and led him along the stone wall. In the total blackout, touch was her only guide and the sound of their breathing disturbed the quiet of the cavern. The temperature was cooler now, the air fresher. The gurgle of running water lifted her spirits, and hope crept into her mind.

As they continued to plod along, the moisture on the wall coated her hand and the sound of rushing water grew louder. Within minutes, her shoes were soaked, and the icy liquid rose above her ankles. Momentarily, the flowing water came up to their hips and Sherry's head brushed the top of a tunnel.

There was a stream from outside that emptied beneath the cavern floor. Something was definitely weird. Streams ran out of mountains, not into them. The fact that it was totally dark here didn't bode well, either. This meant that the top of the tunnel and the water level must meet. Sherry surmised that Ben and Cindy escaped this way before the microbe destroyed their minds. The good news was that Cadence and Sherry had avoided the trap in the moat. The bad news was that she was a one-hundred-pound woman trying to help a really big man.

They moved forward and the frigid current rose to their chests. Finally, the space between the top of the stream and the tunnel shrank to a few inches. Without warning, her confidence hemorrhaged when a decade's old memory surfaced. Sherry was thirteen and waiting by the swimming pool for her lifesaving test score. The instructor had marched down the line of students and gave each one their results. When he got to Sherry, he looked her dead in the eye and growled, "Whittington, if someone's drowning, call for help."

The current pushed against them as she grimaced from the memory. Sherry placed her hand on Cadence's back to steady him and lied for all she was worth. "I'll get you out of here, I promise. Take a deep breath and start prayin'."

Cadence was still half conscious from the blow to his head, so Sherry turned him until his back was against her right side. With her left palm securely under his chin, she pinched his nostrils shut with her fingers. Pulling him under water, she wished she had paid more attention during that damn lifesaving class.

The air space above them was gone and the brisk current slowed their motion. She fought the rapid flow of water by alternately swimming and kicking off the bottom. But when she was starting to feel comfortable, her hand slipped from under Cadence's chin. She groped in the black water until she brushed against his arm. Sherry planted a merciless grip on his chin and prayed he hadn't breathed.

Fifteen or twenty seconds had passed since they started and Sherry felt the burn in her lungs. Her heart hammered in her chest and her muscles cramped from the cold. Pulling Cadence farther into the tunnel, she was dying for air. It was impossible to see, but as they churned along, the darkness slowly brightened. That was a good sign, however, for the second time she had doubts about getting Cadence out. An image of Lightfeather flashed in her mind and she knew if he were in her place, he'd move heaven and earth to save both Cadence and herself. With grim determination, she ignored the pain in her lungs and kept on swimming.

Her lungs were on fire, the pressure to breathe overwhelming. The light in the water continued to brighten and there was only fifteen feet to go. Her kicks were weak and her grip on Cadence's chin weakened. She clawed the water with her free hand to drag them forward.

Ten feet to go.

Ungodly pain shot through her thighs. Her heart thudded out of control. She shuddered and fought the impulse to breathe.

Five feet to go.

The tunnel curved upward into the land-based stream and the strong current slowed their motion.

One foot to go.

They were just inches from the surface and Sherry was totally exhausted. Seconds from defeat, she pulled Cadence close to her body and thought, *we are so screwed.*

And then they surfaced.

CADENCE AND SHERRY ERUPTED UPWARD with a splash, spitting water while the rushing stream swirled around them. Cadence's eyes opened wide. His face was unnaturally white, and he trembled from the frigid water. Sherry held his head above the flowing stream and moved him toward the bank.

Cadence crawled across the rocky bottom and collapsed on dry land. He spit water out and gasped for air. "That was too damn close for me."

His face told Sherry what she already knew.

They were both lucky to be alive.

PUFFY THE TOAD

PUFFY CRAMMED THE LAST FISTFUL of greasy potato chips into his mouth and grunted from sheer delight. Sitting behind the counter in the Aztec service station, he yawned and stared out the window at the Interstate. The station, located on I-25 and the Springer, New Mexico exit, was shunned by the citizens of Springer partly because the service sucked, but mostly because gasoline was thirty cents a gallon higher. Puffy's boss, who also sold pot out of his office, openly bragged about gouging the Interstate's travelers.

Totally bored, Puffy threw the empty sack on the floor and picked up the *Hustler* magazine behind the counter. Porn Stars of California, Page 35, grabbed his attention and he thumbed through the magazine, leaving oily smears on the pages. Stopping at page 32, he sighed and loosened his belt, grunting as his stomach ballooned outward. Puffy eyed a three-page spread about Cheryl and her amazing blender, effectively drawing out the sexual anticipation. But when he turned to page 35, a car pulled into the drive, ringing the station bell.

"Of all the fuckin' times." Standing, he shoved his greasy hand down his pants and adjusted himself as he waddled out the door. A nondescript Mercury came to a stop and the driver's side door opened. Puffy nearly choked when a tall blond stepped onto the drive and into his fantasies. Dressed in skintight, black spandex, she had killer legs, narrow hips, and cupcake breasts.

"W—what'll it be?" he stammered, suddenly self-conscious .

"Fill it with unleaded and check the oil."

The deep voice and her reptilian green eyes should have registered, but he was too far gone with the effect of spandex on a smokin' hot body.

She gave him a cold glance and grabbed a bag from the front seat. "I need to change. Where's the restroom?"

"Uh, inside, on the right."

Puffy licked a broken chip from the corner of his mouth and watched her butt swing as she walked inside. His hands shook when he turned the pump on and shoved the nozzle in the tank. Setting the trigger on automatic, he looked up and down the deserted Interstate. Not a car in sight. Puffy narrowed his eyes and knew timing was everything. He had to be damned quick.

The sweat beaded on his forehead as he scurried into the storeroom. He quietly lifted a case of oil from the rack and removed a small plug in the wall. With his arms resting on the shelf and his butt in the air, he peered into the women's restroom. A quick look around and he knew he'd hit pay dirt. Puffy couldn't believe his luck. The sizzling blond was admiring herself in the full-length mirror and began peeling off the spandex. Lustrous black material part-ed down the front to reveal unbelievably firm, white flesh. She stepped out of the skin-tight fabric, and her back was facing him, but from her reflection in the mirror Puffy had a full-frontal view. Small pink nipples jutted upward and her white complexion made him lick his lips.

Then she shifted her stance by moving her legs apart. Puffy gazed down-ward to her hairless crotch and his heart thudded out of control. His mind broke into a thousand pieces. Something registered in his lust-filled state. Puffy blinked his eyes and looked again. He pinched the bridge of his nose, trying to make sense of it, telling himself it wasn't so. He'd never seen anything like it. Not even in *Hustler*. But right there, in her full-length reflection, were two perfectly formed... *things*. He choked on his surprise. "Oh my God. She's a chick and she's got a *dick.*"

As he moved closer to the peephole, his elbow nudged a can of oil off the shelf. The container crashed to the floor, rolled across the concrete, and thudded against the wall.

Puffy leaned back, seconds from cardiac arrest. Sweat poured down his back, yet, a mixture of fear and excitement drew him back to the peephole. Her clothes were piled in the middle of the floor, but she'd disappeared.

Alarm bells went off in his mind. He'd better get his fat ass out of here, soon. Puffy figured she was dressing out of his line of sight and was confused over this man-woman thing. Confused, and also titillated. He looked over his shoulder, but the storeroom door was still closed. Taking a shaky breath, he wondered, where is she?

He moved into position again, elbows jacked up on the oil rack, his trembling butt high in the air, and waited. And waited some more. Without warning, something slammed into him from behind, and his lungs exploded with a rush of air. His ears roared, and a thousand stars sparkled behind his eyes. Excruciating pain ripped through his balls. He jerked his head around and saw the stunning nude hermaphrodite behind him. Her mouth widened in a dazzling smile.

Puffy was in big trouble.

She flipped her blond hair back and the smile disappeared. "How charming. A fat little peeper."

Puffy hadn't been to church in years, but he suddenly found religion. After some righteous prayer, he stammered, "I didn't mean to do it."

"Of course you didn't," she purred, rearranging his balls in her clenched fist.

Puffy gagged and pain rocketed through his mind. His legs trembled. He almost peed his pants.

"You naughty boy, I caught you peeking," her voice was low and mean.

Puffy closed his eyes and hoped this was a bad dream. But nightmares never hurt like this.

"So, did you like it?"

His jaw quivered. "No."

Her fist tightened, and he sucked in air.

With the fervor of one who's seen the light, he ejaculated the words, "Yes, I did," Puffy whimpered. "In a strange kinda way."

"Telling the truth make it better?"

Puffy tried to nod yes.

"What's your name, peeper?"

"Billy Toed. Everyone calls me Puffy." Another problem was about to surface, and the blood drained from his face. The stress inside hit critical mass and he gripped the shelf with both hands. He silently mouthed the words, please, not now, but his head involuntarily tilted downward and the skin under his jaw puffed up. Air rushed from his lungs and his vocal cords vibrated. A loud, *"CROAK,"* echoed inside the small room.

She laughed. "Now you're a fat little toad."

"I can't help it. When I get nervous, it just happens." Puffy trembled and the tears rolled down his cheeks.

The bitch's grip was murderous, and his balls ached like hell.

She asked, "Let's share some quality time Puffy. When did it first happen? The croaking?"

He gritted his teeth from the pain. "First grade. Mrs. Truman's class."

"And?"

"She called on me. Asked what letter came after M. I hadn't been paying attention, and I froze. She yelled at me, called me stupid. When the class laughed, I puffed up and croaked." He hung his head. "Like a toad."

Morda's nipples tightened in sexual arousal as the psychic pain rolled off of Puffy. A sigh escaped her lips as she pinched her hardened nipple between thumb and forefinger. "What happened next?"

Puffy tried to lick his lips, but his mouth was desert dry. "It wasn't over. At recess, the kids made a circle around me and yelled, Billy Toad, Billy Toad. And… and then my best friend screamed, 'He's a Puffy Toad.'" Puffy shook from the memory and whimpered in shame, "He gave me that nickname and never lets me forget it. But the bitchin' part is, he's my boss now."

The silence in the storeroom was deafening. Sweat poured down his face and he listened to it drop on the shelf. Outside, a semi rig roared down the interstate and faded away.

PUFFY'S SHAME AND DEGRADATION FRACTURED something inside Morda, shattering the barrier to a forgotten past. A thousand shards slashed her psyche, revealing disturbing fragments of her childhood. For the first time since that bitter day, Morda remembered her true name.

Jimmy Tate.

It was a hot summer morning, and eight-year-old Jimmy squirmed in the front seat of a '78 Chevy. The windows were rolled up and the stench of sweat and liquor rolled off of Grandpa Bones. Yet there was something else in the air, something Jimmy didn't quite understand.

He looked out the window at the city park, then down at the dress he'd been forced to put on. His eyes rolled up and he trembled. "But I'm not a girl."

Grandpa backhanded him and leaned so close that Jimmy smelled his reeking breath. "Yes, you are," he slurred. Pulling a tube of lipstick from his pocket, he smeared it across Jimmy's lips. "If you're gonna be a girl, you gotta look like one."

Shoving the passenger door open, he said, "I promised your Momma I'd take you to the park today. And lookey there, your friends are waitin' on ya." Grandpa waved his hand toward the five young boys at the picnic table. "Now you can show 'em what you really are."

Jimmy put his hands over his head. "I don't wanna do it."

Grandpa took a pull on his whiskey bottle and shoved Jimmy out of the car. "This ain't the worst that's gonna happen," he promised in a crazy whine.

Jimmy slunk toward the picnic bench, wishing he were dead. With his head bowed, he stopped in front of his second-grade friends. The moment they recognized him, their kinetic chatter died. Five faces twisted with astonishment and nervous laughter spread among them.

His best friend, Mike, raised his brow. "Why you wearin' a dress, Jimmy? An' what you got lipstick on for?"

Jimmy stared at the ground and scuffed the dirt with his pink shoe.

Mike cried, "You a sissy boy, Jimmy! So, where's your dolly? Anybody wearin' a dress needs a dolly."

The other boys laughed and moved closer.

Jimmy glanced back at the car and his face burned with humiliation. Tugging at the dress he was wearing, he knew if he ran away, Grandpa's rage would be worse than what his friends would do.

In unspoken unison, the boys formed a circle. Mike swaggered closer, towering over Jimmy. The bully pointed his finger, and said, "We're gonna take you down sissy boy. And we'll pull your panties off."

"No! Don't do it." Jimmy screamed. But Mike tackled him and the others pinned him to the ground. He struggled and nearly freed himself until Mike punched him in the stomach.

"Damnit, that's the way I like it," Mike shrieked. "Let's see what he's got."

The twisted canopy of elm trees above Jimmy formed a writhing mosaic as the wind violated the leaves. The abrasive sound of nearby traffic mixed with the jubilant whoops of his tormentors—until the cotton panties came off.

Mike pointed, "Oh shit. Guys, look at this."

The other four let go and crowded around Jimmy's open legs. Their young faces reflected naive fascination, before twisting to dark revelation.

Mike spit out, "He's a boy… and a girl."

In total disgust, Mike threw the panties on Jimmy's face and turned his back in contempt.

Jimmy felt the wind lick his bare legs and thighs. The last thing he remembered was gasping for air.

MORDA'S TORTURED BREATHING STOPPED WHEN she responded to Puffy. "Children are animals with a natural talent for cruelty. I understand your pain because I'm different too. I heard their taunts and wasn't strong enough to fight back. There were always too many of them. But when you get older, you find ways to get even. I'm no longer weak, Puffy, but you are. Pathetically so."

Her soft, evil laugh raised the hairs on Puffy's neck.

"Don't think we're bonding, Puffy. Far from it. My decision to let you go surprises me. Let's just say I'm in a generous mood today. I've done a lot of bad things in my life, but even in the darkest of souls, there's a glimmer of light."

She loosened her grip around his balls. "You gonna let me go?"

Morda made Puffy a solemn promise. "Yes, and I'm going to do something even better. I'm going to burn this fucking building to the ground."

Puffy started to rise and she squeezed again.

His legs wobbled and he let out a tremendous, *"CROAK."*

Having made her point, Morda let go. "I'm going to gather my things, Puffy. And when I leave the restroom, I want you to run for your life. If you try to identify me when the police come, I will find you. And my appetite for revenge is beyond imagination. If you tell anyone about me, we'll bond in ways too horrible to imagine. Am I *clear?"*

As she left the room, Puffy choked out a pitiful, "Yes." For two agonizing minutes, he listened to his heart hammering in his chest. He sucked in deep breaths and felt the pain ease in his balls but was damned if he'd look through the peephole again. He waited until her car door slammed outside. Puffy wobbled a few painful steps and stumbled from the storeroom. Gathering momentum, he crashed through the back door and ran into the vast field behind the station. The breath jerked from his lungs and he gained speed, running for his life, past small cactus and through knee high grass. From the corner of his eye, he saw six pump nozzles spewing gas across the driveway. Ten feet from the spreading liquid, the Mercury was idling on the edge of the pavement. The She-Male's hand emerged from the driver's window, dropping a burning paper to the ground. The car burnt rubber and rocketed down the asphalt when the gasoline was feet from the flame. Puffy clenched his fists and swung his arms, gaining five yards before the explosion slammed his body. Heat singed his hair and scorched his exposed skin. The smoke and fire mushroomed upward, and he screamed in exhilaration. Running across the prairie while the station burned, he was free for the first time since Mrs. Truman's class.

MORDA STARED AT THE BILLOWING fire in the car's rearview mirror and experienced a profound liberation. She'd reclaimed a part of her hidden past when she unearthed young Jimmy Tate, but the disturbing question of how and when she became Morda was still a mystery. She yearned to uncover the events of her past, yet she fought with an internal voice that whispered, *fuck it, you've got shit to do.*

She sped through the small town of Springer, New Mexico and the houses flashed by, giving way to wide open plains. The hum of the tires on the road ripened into a whine when she pushed the car to one-hundred miles an hour. The final piece of Morda's past beckoned, hovering on the edge of awareness. She feared the disturbing answer would appear all too soon.

THE CLOCK IS TICKING

SHERRY WOBBLED TO HER FEET and rubbed her arms and legs to fight the numbing cold. "Are you okay, Cadence?"

"Aside from the ball-freezing water and a blow to the head, yeah. I'm doing better, but we need a plan to intercept Morda."

"You're in no shape to move," she said, "so I'll go around, pick up the vehicle, and come back for you. Then we'll haul ass to the Angel Fire airport. They have a charter service there. You wouldn't happen to be a pilot, would you?"

"I am, but I can't fly. Not when my body could shut down from Morda's drug." He glanced at his watch, "If what she told us is true, we have an hour before I lose my motor control."

"I'd better hoof it back to the Jeep."

Cadence pitched Sherry the keys. "Run like your life depends on it. Because mine does."

SHE WAS BACK WITH CADENCE'S Jeep in twenty minutes and skidded to a stop by the stream. "We got lucky because Morda left your vehicle intact. Crawl in, strap on your seat belt, and let's get the hell out of here."

Cadence lumbered inside, and Sherry felt the loud boom of thunder when the rain started pouring down. She ground the gears into first and bulldozed her way through the narrow ruts that lead down the mountain. "How are you doing, Cadence?"

He turned his face up to the mirror and Sherry saw the muscles tense in his jaw. Her intuition told her that things were not good, because he didn't comment. She met his gaze in the mirror, and said, "It'll work out, Cadence. I just have a feeling." Sherry heard the tension in her voice and it screamed, "liar."

Cadence's gaze flickered between the road and the mirror, missing nothing.

Sherry leaned over and put her hand on his muscled shoulder. "We'll get to the ranch before Morda does."

The disbelief in Cadence's eyes was palpable as she downshifted and gunned the engine, making her own path down the mountain. Pine branches whipped across the windshield and raked the body of the Jeep when they plowed through small trees and thick brush. Minutes later, the rain fell in a solid sheet and they broke into a small clearing.

A red metal bar blocked the exit out of the forest.

The rain pummeled their vehicle and the high-speed action of the Jeep's wipers barely cleared the windshield. Inside their cramped space, Sherry recognized the tang of her own fear and desperation. Time was running out and she needed to move.

Cadence turned around and stared through her.

"Put this bitch in gear. Ram it."

Sherry red lined the engine and popped the clutch. The front bumper slammed the barrier. The wheel jerked from her hands and the gate crashed open. She regained control and careened down the path leading back to the highway. Her only thought was reaching Lightfeather in time.

HOT TIME IN THE OLD TOWN

MORDA GLANCED AT HER GPS on the outskirts of Clayton, New Mexico. Just three hours separated her from this desolate town and the Whittington's ranch. Even though the promise of impending violence against Lightfeather should have lifted her spirits, the disturbing connection with young Jimmy bothered her.

Morda couldn't repress her anger when she relived Jimmy's humiliation in the park. That defining moment was a dark blade that twisted her soul on too many levels. But she knew there was more. Much more. Unfortunately, the missing link of how she became Morda put her on the brink of mental implosion.

The solution unfolded when she saw the Truck Stop. Its immense parking lot was nearly vacant with only a few vehicles in front of the restaurant. Driving to the opposite end of the lot, she stopped and put the car in park.

This was what she had in mind.

She lifted the velvet pouch from the passenger's seat. Removing the crystal skull taken from beneath the Sphinx's paw, she watched tiny reflections of light play upon its polished surface, producing murky, fleeting images that ebbed and flowed. The empty hollows where the eyes should have been radiated a dark energy that gripped her gut. For in the center of each orbit were two identical images. The twin reflections were part Morda, and part something else. Something hideous and strange. Much like a funhouse mirror that distorted reality, it created a twisted caricature of her that amazed and horrified. She looked deeper into the visual difference and formed the question, who am I?

The twin reflections faded away and bone chilling cold blasted through the skull, stinging her hands. The quest for truth had awakened its ancient power.

The skull's weight lessened, growing exponentially lighter until it floated in the air, even with the dash. Strangely, the skull did not open into halves as it had for the archeologist at the Sphinx. This time, the eye sockets filled with an azure liquid that funneled downwards to the base of the skull. The vibrant substance streamed in an arterial flow, gushing across the carpet in a silent wave, coating the floorboards and the seat where Morda sat. It silently oozed up the doors and windows, then across the roof.

The shimmering essence had no warmth or wetness and covered the interior surface of the car, cocooning Morda in a dark, energized womb that pulsed with intelligent life.

An unearthly cold filled the car and a plume of vapor came from Morda's lips when she spoke the words, "Who am I?"

In response, the deep blue womb spewed spider webs of ancient darkness that crackled and shimmered. Dark tendrils pulsed and writhed with manic force, blossoming into demonic energy, until the interior of the car was black as the heart of death.

A pinpoint of light expanded from within the darkness and spread across the car's interior to reveal young Jimmy pinned to the ground by his five friends. Morda's gut tightened as she connected with Jimmy's soul because the pain was amplified. She sensed the individual cruelty of her tormentors as they held Jimmy down. When they tore Jimmy's panties off, she felt their utter contempt.

Gratefully, the scene ended and Morda stared once more into the black heart of this voyeuristic womb. Ironically, the bitter seed to her identity had been planted that day in the mind of Jimmy Tate. When the black screen shimmered once more, Morda's heart pounded in her chest. The origin of her name would now be revealed.

A stab of fear shot through Morda when she recognized the inside of her mother's two room apartment. Jimmy lay curled on his soiled mattress sucking the collar of his pajama top while faint sunlight filtered through the room's torn curtains. While Jimmy stared at the rats fighting for crumbs on the kitch-en floor, he vaguely remembered Mother coming home before going to her second job. Anxiety filled him and he wondered if she was aware of what had happened in the park today. In the darkest part of his heart, he knew she did and she didn't even care.

The bedsprings creaked in the other room and Jimmy held his breath, listening to the slow, sandpaper shuffle of bare feet on a dirty floor. It meant only one thing.

Grandpa was awake.

The raspy movement stopped. Jimmy's eyes widened when the old man's hands thrust through a hole in the wall.

It was over one-hundred degrees in the stifling apartment, yet Jimmy's body went cold.

"Come here, bitch. I got something for ya," Grandpa whispered in a drunken slur.

The boy cringed in terror. "No!"

"You'll come if ya know what's good for ya."

Jimmy jerked upward, frantic to escape. The deadbolt on the door was locked and the key nowhere in sight. Glancing at the room's only window, he felt a glimmer of hope. Easing off the stained mattress, he tiptoed across the floor and pushed up on the window.

Grandpa chuckled.

The window was stuck.

"Ain't nowhere to go, Jimmy." Grandpa gestured with his wrinkled hands. "So git your ass over here."

The back of his neck prickled, and he took a faltering step toward the hole.

Sensing his hesitation, Grandpa cackled. "I'll beat ya and your Momma if ya don't come here."

A cloud outside obscured the afternoon sunlight and the room darkened. Jimmy moved closer. He observed the spidery veins and sores on the back of Grandfather's hands before they closed around his head.

Jimmy clenched his eyes shut and leaned into the opening.

After a few minutes, the old man rasped, "This ain't all that's gonna happen.

'Cause there's more, much more, to come." Hideous laughter erupted from the old man's throat and he shoved Jimmy away.

Self-loathing and hatred consumed Jimmy when he fell onto the littered floor. He rolled to his side, gagging from shock and horror. Pieces of trash stuck to his face and he gripped his sides, sobbing. He tried to grasp what had just happened. His fragile mind shattered and a bitter seed blossomed into unholy rage. His body shook as he balled his fists. He silently vowed that he'd never be powerless again.

The bedsprings in the next room groaned when Grandpa collapsed in a drunken heap.

Jimmy waited for the old man's breathing to deepen before opening his own eyes. He drew a harsh breath when he saw a large rat standing on its hind legs, sniffing the air. Its tiny whiskers twitched and it squeaked in defiance, glaring at him with red eyes. Burning hatred exploded inside of him, and his hand shot out like a whip, catching the rat by the throat. He slowly tightened his grip.

The rat's neck snapped, and Jimmy squeezed even harder, relishing its dying spasms. When the rodent stopped jerking, he dropped the carcass and narrowed his eyes. A simple plan formed, and Jimmy knew it required all the courage he had. Before he could change his mind, he quickly stripped off his pajamas and donned the dress, shoes, and panties Grandfather had hidden in the dresser.

Jimmy looked at his reflection in the cracked mirror. His thin arms and legs were frail. He knew he was young and weak, but when he turned to either side and studied his reflection, he realized the meaning of the word chameleon. What better way to disguise himself than to take on the clothing and manner of a little girl? He'd always been an astute observer of human nature. By watching the other children on the playground, he knew the girls were written off as a nuisance by the boys. Yet when the young females wanted something from their male targets, charm, flattery, and misdirection delivered the spoils into their hands.

With mounting sureness, he entered Grandfather's bedroom and listened to him snore for a moment. Jimmy grabbed the door key on the nightstand, bent down, and turned on the electric heater by the bed. The fan motor rattled to life and blew air across five red hot coils. He strode back to the kitchen and kicked at the remaining rats before he opened the oven door. Twisting all the valves wide open, pungent gas spewed into the room.

Jimmy took one last look around. The mirror cast a dark reflection of his new identity before he unlocked the door and stepped outside. He set the deadbolt with a satisfying click. Walking down the sidewalk, Jimmy choked out the words, "More to come."

Five minutes later, a burden lifted from his shoulders when he heard the explosion and saw the flames. For the first time that day, he smiled. In his new identity as a chameleon, he would don the cloak of the lamb to disguise the savagery of the lion. Even though he didn't know where he was going, or how he was going to live, he now had a name.

It was a name that would bring pain and suffering to those who heard it. For his victims, there would always be more, morda come.

On that hot summer's day, the hideous seed planted in the soul of Jimmy Tate gave birth to the monster called Morda. Morda Comm.

Inside the Mercury, the voyeuristic screen faded to dark blue and she smiled in satisfaction. In the semidarkness, she knew that Jimmy's childhood abuse had fueled her rage against society, which in turn had led to her rise in the criminal world where ruthlessness and savagery were valuable commodities. Even though the trauma of her childhood had blocked her early memories, the power of the crystal skull brought her journey from Jimmy Tate to Morda Comm full circle.

When Morda looked down at her pale silk blouse and matching skirt, she knew there was but one true path… and that was the way of the chameleon.

As that thought resonated within her, the dark blue screen inside the car flickered one last time. Like it had for the archeologist in the tunnel beneath the Sphinx, Morda knew the crystal skull would deliver its prophecy of things to come.

The image showed a helicopter high in the sky, careening dangerously from left to right and plummeting downward. While it spun out of control, Morda was perched on the inside ledge of the cargo door.

Just moments from impact, she leaped clear of the plane only to plunge to an inevitable death.

The prophetic image faded and the dark liquid coating the inside of the car receded back into the skull. It slowly lowered to the floorboard on Morda's right.

Brilliant sunlight penetrated the Mercury and Morda reflected upon the image that predicted her future death. With two words, she summed it up nicely. "How interesting."

WHO YOU GONNA CALL?

SHERRY HIT THE ACCELERATOR AND the engine roared, casting its throaty sound inside the Jeep's cramped quarters. She white knuckled the steering wheel and they slid from the muddy mountain road on to slick asphalt. With only a passing thought to safety, she ploughed the vehicle across the pavement and into the right lane. She slammed the stick shift from gear to gear and took the next two miles of hairpin turns at twice the legal limit, dropping nine hundred feet in a matter of minutes.

As they reached the end of the Taos Pass, she looked over and saw the wrinkles in the corners of Cadence's eyes. Even though he didn't smile, she knew he was happy to be alive.

"We're two miles from the airport and it looks like the rain's starting to slow. If the weather's on our side we'll be airborne in fifteen minutes."

She scanned the road and continued, "I've been here before in a private plane and it was two hours from Angel Fire to the Texas Panhandle. With some luck, we'll get there before Morda does."

Sherry bit her bottom lip and the Jeep squealed onto the airport road. The small strip, nestled in a basin surrounded by the magnificent Sangre de Cristo Mountains, was just a stone's throw from the small resort town of Angel Fire. The mountain's Spanish name translated to blood of Christ—a term coined by nineteenth century observers when the sun's crimson glow exploded over the peaks.

Sherry parked by the airport office and opened her door before turning around. "Here's my cell phone. Call Lightfeather and have him contact the Sheriff. Then tell him to get the hell out of there."

With those words, she slammed her door and ran to the office to get a plane.

CADENCE FUMBLED WITH THE PHONE and hurriedly punched in the ranch number. The call connected and there were a series of clicks before a recorded voice informed, *"Service to this area is temporarily down, please try again at a later time."*

"This can't happen now." He slammed the phone against his thigh. Sherry had told him that Morda was devious and had used a Taser to subdue her. Cadence knew Lightfeather was tough and a good judge of people, but he was no match for Morda. When Lightfeather answered the door, she would probably play the helpless female feigning car trouble or needing directions. Lightfeather would never have a chance because as soon as the bitch stepped inside, she'd hit him with the Taser.

Cadence rushed inside, past Sherry and the man she was talking to, and grabbed the cordless phone on the counter. He didn't have time to wait for permission so he punched in Lightfeather's number. Rain and sweat coated his forehead and he swayed from side to side from the recent blow to his head. The pre-recorded message said, *"No service available."* Pain shot through his temple as his world imploded.

SHERRY NODDED AND ACKNOWLEDGED THE bad news. "There's a violent storm and all communication lines are down."

She reached out and took the phone from Cadence's hand. "That means we're stuck here until it clears."

Sherry presented their only option to Bob, the airport manager, "Can we use the radio in the plane?"

"You could, but you'd have to reach twelve thousand feet to contact the FAA at Albuquerque Center. Once you do, you could deliver a message."

There was steel in Bob's eyes and confidence in his message. He ran a hand through his hair and she sensed his true character. He was a man who helped those in need and gave his best effort to be a game changer. A crooked grin spread across Bob's face and hope flickered inside Sherry.

He rubbed his whiskers and looked at Cadence. "From what Sherry told me, you two need a ride back to the Texas Panhandle in a bad way."

"That's putting it lightly." Cadence dipped his head respectfully. "We're desperate to get back. A man's life depends on it."

"You just hit the lotto, because I'm a pilot and my plane is ready for hire. The Angel Fire weather can change quickly. When it clears up we'll be ready to fly. Once we reach the right altitude, we'll make that call."

The variables ran through her head. How fast was Morda driving? Would the rain lift in time? How long would it take the Sheriff to reach Lightfeather?

Bob crossed his arms, "Don't worry about it, Sherry. I'll get the plane prepped and ready to fly. If we get in the air sooner, I'll radio ahead."

A gust of wind rattled the building as heavy rain slammed against the roof. Sherry had skied Angel Fire before and knew how changeable the mountain weather could be. Because he was an experienced pilot, Bob understood that too. Yet what impressed her most about him was that he remained calm and positive. His striking blue eyes and unflinching gaze conveyed a sense of strength and resolve. He had no idea how much that meant to her. She lifted her head and said, "Let's get the plane ready and pray for a break."

ALBUQUERQUE CENTER

THE FORCE OF THE REVVED engine vibrated their 1968 Cessna and Bob listened to the engine's pulse. Evidently pleased with the results, he released the brake and taxied onto the runway. Over the roar of the engine, he announced on the airport frequency, "Angel Fire Traffic, November four six niner six Tango moving on to 17 for immediate departure, southbound to Las Vegas, New Mexico."

Bob applied power and the force pushed Sherry back into the copilot's seat. Once the old Cessna gained momentum and reached sixty miles per hour, the nose began to rise as the plane gently lifted from the asphalt.

As they climbed steadily upward, they were sandwiched between the ground and the low hanging clouds, making their way south through the mountain pass. On both sides were several peaks, the tops of which were shrouded by mist. Bob spoke to Sherry through her headphones, "We've got about fifteen hundred feet between the ground and the clouds, so this trip is doable."

Even though Cadence was still mentally aware and strapped in the back seat, worry and frustration ate at her soul. Unfortunately, irony reared its scaly head and rubbed her face in the one thing she couldn't change—Lightfeather's fate was out of her hands and would be decided by how quickly they got to the ranch.

Bob didn't know all the details about their situation, but he knew enough to bring a wicked looking Colt .45 semiautomatic gun. Sherry recognized the vintage World War II weapon from the one Lightfeather kept in his ranch truck. The same one he had taught her to break down, clean, and shoot when she was younger.

Much to her mother's horror.

Even though Sherry could go after Morda with a gun, she was out of her league and would end up dead. There was an overwhelming evil about Morda that a stake to her heart couldn't cure. It was thirty minutes past the psychopath's deadline, promising lights out for Cadence. Sherry ruled out his help, but she was confident Bob could wield the business end of his .45. It seemed the odds were finally in their favor.

The sudden crackle of static in Sherry's headphones roused her and she leaned forward. Bob spoke over the radio, "Albuquerque Center, this is November four six niner six Tango requesting flight following."

Sherry took a deep breath.

There was nothing but static, so Bob repeated the call a second time. He gave a worried shake of his head. "Our problem is low altitude and the high mountains. Both of which won't allow radio contact with Albuquerque." Bob checked his gauges. "This radio is an older model and isn't that reliable, so we might not be able to call for help at all."

Sherry did the logistics in her mind and spoke into the headset microphone, "The person we're after isn't one who plays by the rules, so I know the bitch won't drive the speed limit. With her increased speed, I put her about ninety minutes from the ranch. We've been in the air a quarter hour now, so we'll get there fifteen minutes after she does." Fear constricted her heart and she prayed for a miracle.

Bob knew the score and pushed the throttle all the way in. The old engine delivered a few more miles per hour. "I'll get everything out of the plane and whittle her lead down by five minutes." He acknowledged their bad situation. "It's the best I can do Sherry."

"That'll leave Morda alone with Lightfeather for ten minutes," she said in a voice too low to hear.

Just a few hours ago, the incredible wave of luck she'd ridden allowed her to escape death on two separate occasions. Then it placed Bob in her path. A man who wasn't afraid to get involved and took pride in doing what was right.

But her streak of good fortune was stretched mighty thin now. It came down to fifteen minutes. Fifteen minutes to determine whether someone she'd placed in the path of a homicidal monster would live.

Or die.

HANGING BY A
THREAD

THEY FLEW THREE HUNDRED FEET above the ground and were closing in fast on the ranch house. Despair wrapped its gnarled fist around Sherry's chest and squeezed her hope away—all because of a time-consuming head wind.

She knew if Morda got there first, her fifteen-minute lead would not be terminal for Lightfeather. Morda was one who liked to toy with her prey and screw with their minds. But, because of their delay, the bitch would have been alone with him for twenty-five minutes. That spelled catastrophe.

To whittle away at Morda's edge, Bob was setting down on the caliche road leading to the house, rather than the landing strip a quarter mile away.

As they got closer to the house, Sherry didn't see any suspicious cars parked in front and she prayed they had arrived first. A man's life was at stake here—a precious man whom she couldn't bear to lose.

Tears seeped from the corners of her eyes and she finally took a deep breath when the plane's wheels bit into the rutted road. She was overwhelmed with raw emotion as memories of Lightfeather's unconditional love emerged. Those emotions couldn't help her now and she banished her thoughts to a dark and sterile corner. In its place, she steeped in the bitterness of anger. Sherry blamed herself for endangering the most important person in her life, Lightfeather.

She looked at Bob for reassurance while he taxied down the white caliche road. His face was battle hard and his lips compressed into a cold, narrow slit. They pulled up to the front of the house and his blue eyes were serious and very scary.

He killed the engine and grabbed his .45. "Stay here, Sherry. I'm going to check inside."

Bob threw his door open and hit the muddy ground running. He sprinted across the parking area, pounded up the concrete sidewalk, and leaped onto the porch. He looked into the widow, leveled his automatic, and rushed inside.

Even though Sherry had no love for Morda, may God have mercy on her if she got in Bob's way. That bitch was about to face one badass machine.

Fifteen minutes ago, Cadence had slipped into the predicted coma, and Sherry fidgeted with indecision. The logical part of her mind dictated that it was safer in the plane, but she was the one who had gotten Lightfeather in this mess. She had to do something, so she ignored Bob's order and jumped out.

She scanned the parking area in front of her and something odd caught her eye. Faint outlines in the mud showed imprints of a car pulling in and backing out. That unmistakable detail birthed a really bad feeling, causing Sherry's thoughts to shift into gear. She knew Morda had already been here.

And gone.

A horrific scream came from the darkened workshop, shaking her to the core. Bob was still inside the house, and Sherry didn't have time to get to him. She scrambled up the concrete drive and rushed through the workshop door. It was nearly pitch-black inside and she heard, "Oh sweet Jesus. What's she done to my baby?"

It was Leitha's desperate plea.

Sherry's eyes adjusted to the darkness, and she made out Leitha's abundant body, covered with an oversized tee shirt. She had a muddy, pink bunny rabbit slipper on her right foot and her face twisted with fear.

Blood was splattered across the garage floor and tools scattered across the shop. The whites of Leitha's eyes shone against her mahogany skin and she clutched Lightfeather's legs to her chest.

But something was wrong. Leitha was standing and embracing Lightfeather's thighs.

Sherry couldn't comprehend the scene until she looked at the wooden rafters above. The faint outline of a taut rope trailed downward and ended in a loop around Lightfeather's neck.

His eyes bulged, and he was hanging by the neck two feet above the floor.

Fear twisted Sherry's heart.

Guilt rushed through her soul.

Lightfeather was dead. And it was all her fault.

JUST MINUTES
BEFORE....

MORDA KILLED THE MERCURY'S ENGINE in front of the ranch house and frowned at the muddy parking area. In true form, she accepted the tribulations one had to endure to get a job done, but she'd be damned if she'd muddy her Jimmy Choo sandals in the process.

Quickly donning a pair of white Nikes, she glanced in the mirror to check her hair and lipstick. Pure dynamite. Morda knew the effect would probably be lost on Lightfeather, but she did have standards.

Now that the rain had stopped, a feeling of anticipation lifted her frown into a smile.

Lightfeather, you're in for a big surprise.

Morda stepped outside and the mud sucked at her Nikes as she sloshed across the lot. She left a trail of muddy tracks while she walked up the sidewalk. Still dressed in a pale silk blouse and matching skirt, she hurried onto the porch clutching a blue Prada purse in her hand.

Morda knocked on the wooden edge of the screen door and peered into the living room. It definitely lacked a feminine touch because the décor was sparse and too practical for her tastes.

She took a deep breath. The closeness of impending violence always triggered an adrenaline surge. A rush that enhanced her senses to the point of hyper acuity, allowing her to hear the faint creak of wooden flooring in the back hallway. The subtle smell of oil and gasoline affirmed her suspicion. Lightfeather strode into the living room.

He was an imposing figure dressed in faded Levis and a sweatshirt. Standing over six feet tall, Lightfeather was well muscled and had his long silver hair tied in a ponytail. Interestingly, his eyes reflected layers of deep intelligence and were enhanced by an eerie spiritual presence.

He stopped behind the screen door, crossed his arms, and furrowed his brow.

Morda coyly turned her eyes away when he rumbled, "Don't get many guests here. What can I do for you?"

Consummate in the art of deception, Morda crafted herself as an unsure, soft spoken female who needed help. She shifted into a submissive posture and nervously touched her hair. "Hi, I'm Morda and I, I'm sorry to bother you. But I was looking for the Alibates Flint Quarry and got lost. Now my car is on empty."

Lightfeather narrowed his eyes and glanced at her Mercury parked outside.

Lifting her hand to her brow, Morda sighed. "Can you help me?"

The scrutiny faded from Lightfeather's face as he opened the door and stepped onto the porch. "I've got a can of gas in the workshop." He led her down the walkway and through the muddy parking space.

Still in character, Morda walked daintily across the mud, trying to stay in the dry spots while keeping an eye on him. He moved with an athletic grace uncommon for a man in his mid-sixties and exhibited a directness and decisiveness to his motion. Morda knew if he harbored any doubt about her true intentions or identity, he would have telegraphed his emotion. In her state of heightened awareness, she would have sensed his alarm. But this multilayered man emanated only truth and honesty. Two traits that would soon be the death of him.

A kind smile touched his lips and Morda hurried up to him.

"My shoes are absolutely ruined, but I'll take the mud over thumbing a ride to the gas station."

Lightfeather gave a slight nod and they stepped into the murky interior of the shop.

Darkness had always been liberating for Morda because she came alive in the shadows. When something dark and sinister stirred within her, she welcomed the unlikely coupling of evil and creativity that focused her senses.

The building contained an assortment of wrenches, pliers, and screwdrivers suspended on a peg board to her right, and a steel workbench with grinder and vice on the left. Along the back wall of the shop was a Lincoln welding machine, cutting torches, and a large propane tank.

Morda's plan fell into place when she noted a small shop stool alongside a generous length of rope. She looked up at the wooden rafters and her body tingled with excitement.

She reached inside her purse just as Lightfeather glanced at her.

His eyebrows arced upward when he saw what was in her hand.

Morda flipped her blond hair back and smiled impishly. "It's my secret indulgence," she explained. Removing the candy bar, she asked, "Care for some chocolate?"

The chocolate bar slipped from her fingers and she put a hand to her mouth. "How clumsy of me."

Lightfeather's eyes lingered on hers for a moment before he bent to retrieve it.

In the fraction of a second it took Lightfeather to lower his head, Morda reached inside her purse, gripped a small billy club, and slammed it against the base of his skull.

He collapsed on the concrete floor. The force was calculated to momentarily stun, allowing Morda time to grab the nearby rope and throw it over a wooden rafter. She hummed a strain from *Ave Maria*, quickly fashioning a noose and slipping it over Lightfeather's head. Morda cinched the rope around his neck.

Lightfeather began to stir, so she grabbed a three-legged stool and placed it next to his feet. He was coming to when she pulled the other end of the rope and wrapped it around the steel leg of the work bench. With only seconds to spare, she removed a pair of handcuffs from her purse and locked his hands behind his back.

Lightfeather's eyes fluttered and he started to rise. Morda jumped back, jerked on the rope, and hoisted him to his feet. The pang of sexual arousal shot through her groin and she shouted, "Stand up on the stool."

Anger flashed on Lightfeather's face and he thrashed against the rope and handcuffs. But the next words from Morda froze him to the spot.

"Do it now. If you want to keep Sherry alive."

His body shook with rage. "Who the hell are you? And what have you done to her?"

"Get up. Right now. Or she's dead fucking meat."

Lightfeather's face went white and he seemed to age ten years. He reluctantly climbed atop the stool.

Morda took up the slack in the rope and tied it securely to the steel workbench leg. Now that her hands were free, she pulled a Taser from her purse and came back to him. A sliver of laughter erupted from her throat. "You're such a gullible fool."

She put her free hand against the back of his thighs and pushed, shifting his center of balance, causing him to wobble.

His only choice was to allow the rope to tighten around his neck to keep from falling. He teetered on the edge of the stool for several seconds and slowly arced his back in an effort to shift his weight and take the pressure off his neck.

This delicate balancing act wasn't lost on Morda. She admired his ability not to panic and to think logically in the face of possible strangulation.

For now, Morda's intent wasn't to kill, merely intimidate. She clearly had him by the balls.

Lightfeather recovered his balance and took a deep breath. His brow wrinkled with concern, yet his voice was even and calm, "What have you done to Sherry?"

Morda dismissed his question. "Your concern is so touching." A sly smile touched her lips and she rotated a knob on her Taser and held it up. "Did you know there's been a revolution in personal protection devices?" She touched a button on the Taser, and a thick line of blue electricity crackled between two metal poles.

His eyes remained on hers, his face attentive and unaffected.

"Technology is so much fun," Morda commented when she rolled up his left pant leg. She pressed the Taser against his bare flesh and delivered a small jolt of electricity.

He stiffened, yet refused to scream.

"You see," she explained, "I've modified this one so I can adjust the shock to your system."

Morda tapped a slender finger against her lips and said, "Now that we've gotten to know each other, I'm in the mood for a game." She dialed the Taser up a notch. "This is quite simple. I'll ask a question. You'll answer. If the answer isn't right, well... *oops.* "

She laughed and stroked the firm flesh of his exposed leg.

"First question. Do you love Sherry?"

He closed his eyes and spoke softly, "What have you done to her?"

"Oops."

When the shock hit him, Lightfeather's knees buckled and the rope bit into his neck. With his air cut off and his balance compromised, he nearly fell off the stool. Even though the shock to his system was stronger than the first one, he wasn't close to passing out. Momentarily stunned, but not out of the game, he quickly regained his footing.

"Next time," Morda purred, "just answer the question."

Sweat covered his brow and he licked his lips. "Of course I love her. Now tell me, where is she?"

Morda was impressed with his outward composure, but she was more in tune with his inner fear. Now that she had his attention, it was time to toy with his mind. "Do you know where she is?"

"With Cadence in New Mexico."

"Very good," Morda replied. "Is Sherry schizophrenic?"

He hesitated, and she moved the Taser toward his leg. "Chop, chop."

Lightfeather's legs still trembled from the last shock and he shouted, "Yes, she's schizophrenic."

"Very good. Now do you think she took her medication with her?" She pursed her lips. "Tick-tock."

"She can't function without her medicine." He gritted his teeth and shouted, "Damn it, yes. She always takes it with her. Wherever she goes."

Morda glanced at her designer watch. "To borrow an old cliché, time flies when you're having fun. I certainly enjoyed my time with Sherry."

"What did you *do* to her?"

She put her palm against her cheek and her eyes opened wide, "I left her to die in a New Mexican cavern."

Horror rippled across Lightfeather's face.

"The irony is," Morda gloated, "you won't live long enough for it to bother you, because you'll be dead in the next fifteen minutes."

STILL HALF ASLEEP, MOMMA LEITHA reached across the bed for Lightfeather and found it empty. She opened one eye and sighed deeply. Their Sunday afternoon lovemaking was the best part of the weekend and always resulted in a blissful nap afterwards. When they awoke, Lightfeather would slip into the kitchen to make homemade Indian sopapillas from a recipe he'd gotten from his mother in Mexico.

Leitha burrowed deeper into her pillow and listened for the rattling of pots and pans, the slamming of the refrigerator door, and other kitchen sounds. But something didn't sound right. The house was strangely quiet.

She sat up, rubbed her eyes, and called out, "Lightfeather?" When he didn't answer, she got out of bed. It wasn't like him to leave without waking her. Leitha shrugged on his large T-shirt, stepped into her pink bunny rabbit slippers, and tried to ignore her bad feeling.

She walked from the back of the house and stood at the screen door. The back of her neck prickled when she saw a strange car parked outside. But when she heard voices in the workshop, her bad feeling got worse.

Instinct drove her to run from the house, across the muddy lot in her slippers, burying one halfway to China in the muck. Leitha didn't give a damn about anything else as long as Lightfeather was okay. But, when she got to the edge of the shop entrance, she heard a wicked laugh that made her blood go cold.

Leitha looked inside and realized her bad feeling was way off the mark. This was now a nightmare from hell. Lightfeather was standing on the shop stool with a rope around his neck and some skinny bitch was about to load a million volts into his leg. With a damn Taser.

Leitha silently crept up behind the Barbie Doll who was totally consumed with Lightfeather. She grabbed a handful of long blond hair and pulled hard enough to break the bitch's neck and send her ass back to hell, but all she got was a wig in her right hand.

The bald-headed slut turned toward her and curled her lips in a sneer, oblivious to Leitha's one hundred fifty-pound advantage. At an early age, Leitha had cut her teeth fighting in the unforgiving streets of east Amarillo where she learned that size wasn't always the winning factor. No, the key to winning came down to forgetting everything you learned about fighting fair, because it limited your options. When Leitha read the look in her opponent's eyes, she knew they were both on the same page.

"What's yo' name, bitch?"

"Morda. Morda Comm."

"What's that? Some kinda hoe-ass name?"

Leitha focused on Morda's eyes and maneuvered closer, looking for an opening or weakness she could exploit. But mid-step, Morda's frontal kick came out of nowhere, connecting with the top of her chest, stunning her with its speed and force. Leitha's sternum throbbed like hell because Barbie Doll had leveraged her body into it. But it also hurt Leitha's pride because she made the mistake of looking at the bitch's eyes. Morda's gaze had distracted her with something she'd never seen before. No anger or intimidation in that stare, just the dark hole of insanity.

Leitha tried to grab Morda's leg, but Barbie Doll was too quick. The bitch was good, Leitha admitted, but this fight was about to get dirty. She flung the blond wig in Morda's face and pivoted towards the tool rack on the left. Grabbing a heavy pipe wrench in her left hand and a screwdriver in her right, Leitha charged her opponent with the screwdriver high in the air.

Gotcha now, bitch. Morda predictably blocked the downward thrust but failed to deflect a bone breaking blow from the wrench on her forearm. Leitha dropped her weapons and charged forward, slamming her full weight into the skinny bitch, ramming her against the steel edge of the work bench.

The vicious impact didn't affect Barbie Doll. The cunt cupped both hands and slammed them against Leitha's ears, bursting one ear drum and leaving the other ringing badly. Morda thrust the base of her palm into Leitha's nose, smashing the cartilage and splattering them both with blood.

Leitha screamed in rage. Wrapping her arms around Morda, she lifted the slut and rammed her spine against the edge of the work bench, over and over again.

Screeching like a wild animal, Morda gouged Leitha's eyes, but Leitha ducked her head and avoided the assault.

"You gonna die, bitch." Leitha grimaced, lifting Morda high overhead and slammed her into the concrete floor.

Barbie Doll hit the concrete hard but rolled with it and came up on her feet.

The two women squared off, and blood flowed from Leitha's nose and her ruptured eardrum throbbed. Morda bled from numerous cuts as she cradled her broken left forearm.

Leitha looked into Morda's eyes—the dark hole of insanity was still there, but she now showed a dusting of fear. When Leitha moved to cut off Morda's exit, she expected some crazy shit from this cornered animal.

Morda lunged for the Taser at the same time Leitha dived for the pipe wrench. Three feet separated the women and Morda's hand closed around the device. Leitha grabbed the wrench, somersaulted from the dive, and rammed it into Morda's unprotected stomach.

Shock ravaged Morda's face. Staggering across the floor, she doubled over, clutching her stomach. Stepping closer to Lightfeather, she lifted her hands in surrender.

For the first time, Leitha looked up at him, and saw the relief on his face.

Morda was still close to him and bent over. The bitch jerked erect and savagely kicked the base of the three-legged stool, shattering the wood.

Lightfeather plummeted downward. The rope scraped over the rafter above and popped taut, suspending him two feet above the ground.

Leitha balled her fists and screamed. *"Lightfeather."*

Morda shot Leitha an evil glance, grabbed the wig off the floor, and limped from the shop.

Leitha rushed to Lightfeather's side and gripped his legs, trying to hold him up. She looked up at his face and the tears rolled down her cheeks. She cried, "Baby, be strong. I got ya now."

She lifted up Lightfeather's legs but had no idea how long her strength would last.

I WANNA HOLD YOUR HAND

SHERRY STOOD JUST INSIDE THE workshop door—Leitha's mournful cry crushed what was left of her heart. Blood covered the front of Leitha's white T-shirt, and her eyes were glazed from shock. Her nose was slanted to one side and obviously broken.

"Oh sweet Jesus." Leitha held onto Lightfeather's thighs.

Sherry scanned the shop and suppressed a shudder. Tools were scattered across the floor and numerous blood stains were clues to the violent struggle between Morda and Leitha. She noted the shattered stool under Lightfeather and surmised that he was knocked off it by Morda. Leitha had no choice but to try and support Lightfeather's weight until help came.

Sherry rushed to the steel workbench leg and tore at the knot that anchored the rope around Lightfeather's neck. But it was cinched tight from his weight. "Lift him higher."

Leitha grunted from the effort and the cords on her neck jutted out. Struggling to lift him higher, she put her last bit of strength into it. It was just enough to release the tension.

Sherry quickly untied the knot and Leitha collapsed with Lightfeather to the floor. Removing the noose from around his neck, Sherry shook him by the shoulders. "Lightfeather." But he didn't respond. Her hand trembled and she placed her fingers over his carotid artery to check for a pulse.

It was faint and erratic. Sherry prayed it wasn't too late. Tilting his head back, she pinched his nostrils shut and delivered a rescue breath. Lightfeather's chest rose, so she gave four more breaths and checked his pulse again.

A little better. "He's got a regular rhythm, Leitha."

Leitha nodded and finally wiped her bloody nose.

Sherry placed her lips against Lightfeather's and was mentally ambushed when she smelled his aftershave lotion. Her mind went numb. How many times had she smelled that scent? All her life, because it had been as constant and reassuring as the love Lightfeather had given her. A horrible thought surfaced. What if he didn't make it? Dear God, he couldn't die.

Sherry looked at Leitha and took a hit from the pain in her eyes. They were both on the same page with this one. Sherry gave two more sets of five breaths. After the last one, Bob entered the shop and stepped to her side. Both women looked up and saw the grin spreading across his face.

"Doc, I think you've saved the patient."

It didn't register until Sherry looked back at Lightfeather. His eyelids fluttered, and he took a shaky breath.

In a few seconds, his eyes opened wide. He touched the rope burn around his neck. "Sherry. You're not…?"

"Dead?"

He slowly sat up and Sherry threw her arms around him. "I know what Morda told you. I'm so sorry I got you involved in this."

Lightfeather nodded toward his cuffed hands and gave Leitha a wink. She pulled a bobby pin from her hair, bent the end with her teeth, and went to work on the cuffs. In a few seconds she balanced them on the tip of her fingers.

Lightfeather rubbed the deep abrasion on his throat and whispered, "Leitha's had a very broad education." He struggled to stand up and threw his arms around her. "If you weren't such a good street fighter," he rasped out, "I'd be dead." Lightfeather rocked her in a tight embrace and stepped back to look at her face. "I think someone needs to tend to your nose."

"It don't matter about me, sweetie, 'cause you all right now." Suddenly self-conscious, she tugged at the T-shirt and wiped the tears from her eyes. "Gotta say this is one Sunday I won't forget no time soon." Leitha grabbed Lightfeather in a fierce hug and squeezed the air from his lungs. For a few moments they enjoyed the closeness of each other's bodies.

When the moment passed, Leitha sniffled. "Guess I'll go change an' we go to the clinic."

Bob, who had been quietly watching, put his hand on Lightfeather's shoulder. "You should get checked out too."

"I'll do that." He agreed in a hoarse whisper. "When we get back, you and Sherry can tell me what this is all about."

Leitha and Lightfeather turned and walked from the workshop. Sherry was drawn to their obvious differences. He was nearly two feet taller than her and a whole lot lighter. She was African American, and he was Comanche Indian. Even as mismatched as this relationship was, any woman who put her life on the line to save Lightfeather was all good in her books.

Sherry turned and gave Bob a grateful smile. "I have one more request for you. We need to get Cadence to a safe place, which happens to be a local nursing home used by the FBI. I don't have all the details, but they're already caring for two agents involved in this investigation."

She put her hand on Bob's forearm. "There's another car behind the workshop and the keys are in the ash tray. But first, I need a few minutes with Cadence." The shadows were deepening inside the workshop, yet Sherry could see the hard, blue steel of Bob's eyes. She tried to gauge his receptiveness before she explained, "I don't expect you to understand what I'm going to do. In fact, I don't understand how it works. But it does."

Sherry was about to cross a line. On one side was her need to use her psychic ability for good. On the other was her guilt and fear over using it.

They walked out of the workshop in a contemplative silence and crossed the mud to the parked plane. Bob gave her a hand up into the cockpit and waited for her to squeeze in the back with Cadence before he settled into the front seat.

Sherry said, "Bob, just keep an open mind with what I'm going to do." Cadence was slumped against the inside wall and she took his hands in hers. Making sure her fingertips were on his palms, she tried to psychically tune in to his mind. Her voice was clear when she said, "Cadence, I know you can understand me. I'm going to ask you a question, and even though you can't speak, I want you to picture the answer in your mind."

Bob shifted in the front seat and frowned.

Thankfully, he didn't interrupt, so she continued, "When we were in the cavern and the globe showed us the destruction of the ancient civilization, there was a clue to where the crystal was buried."

Numb from exhaustion and stress, Sherry took a deep breath. In order to gain more equanimity, she closed her eyes. "You know where it is because you almost told me before Morda knocked you out. Show me where I need to look."

Images flashed in her mind's eye, yet they didn't have the unique feel she was looking for. There were just random thoughts from her conscious mind. Taking another breath, she repeated, "Show me where the crystal is buried."

This time the image she received hit her on two levels. It came with a feel, or energy, that was apart from her normal consciousness. She received something that was already familiar. The picture she saw in Cadence's mind was a long strip of bare earth.

'A place where nothing grows,' Grandfather had said on his death bed.

The dead zone.

The crystal was buried on Grandfather's ranch. Sherry's body tingled with excitement because she knew it was true. Yet before she closed her psychic connection with Cadence, she had one more question. It was one that he wouldn't willingly give the answer to, so she engaged in mental deceit. Instead of voicing the question, she mentally formed the words in her mind. Who is behind Morda? And who wants the crystal?

The image was so clear and unexpected that she gasped.

Bob leaned across the front seat. "What the hell is going on?"

"You don't want to know." Raw fear bled through her words.

SWEET JESUS AND THE DEVIL

THE MORNING AFTER MORDA'S VIOLENT rampage, Sherry was a total wreck. Yesterday evening, Bob and she took Cadence to the nursing home where Cindy and Ben were cared for. All hell broke loose. The supervisor overseeing Cadence's investigation was called in, and grilled her and Bob about their participation, then Lightfeather and Leitha. It was around three a.m. when he finished, and had put the fear of God into them all. Under no circumstances were they to discuss what had happened amongst themselves or with others.

The supervisor was openly skeptical when Sherry told him she didn't know where the crystal was located. When she lied that Cadence knew but didn't divulge the location, the supervisor bought her story.

Sherry lied for a very obvious reason. After she and Cadence were subdued in the cavern, Morda had said there was a source in the FBI who leaked critical information about the investigation. Sherry don't know how far up the leak went, so she wasn't trusting anyone with the crystal's location. That action alone could land her in jail for a long time, but if the crystal was as dangerous as Sherry believed it was, she would take the chance to keep it out of the wrong hands.

After their inquisition, they all returned to the ranch for a few hours of sleep. Around ten a.m. Sherry gave Bob a hug and her credit card number for the plane ride, along with a heart-felt thanks before he left for New Mexico. Lightfeather took Leitha back to town for a late breakfast and some fresh clothes, after which they would return in a few hours.

All of which fit Sherry's agenda perfectly.

After everyone left, it took her twenty minutes to drive the Caterpillar 416D backhoe from the ranch house to where she thought the crystal was buried. Once she got there, she used a metal detector with the assumption that it was buried in a metal box.

Her shot hit its mark.

Sherry stood next to the backhoe in the center of the area she called the dead zone and climbed into the Caterpillar cab. She twisted the ignition switch, and the seventy-eight- horsepower engine rumbled to life. Turning the driver's seat around, she sat down, and manipulated the controls. The teeth of the bucket bit deep into the barren soil, and it was nice to know she still had the touch.

Over twenty-five years ago, Lightfeather took it upon himself to show her that she could do anything she put her mind to. He taught her how to hunt wild game, weld as good as a man, and play poker with the best of them. Since Grandfather was an oilfield wildcatter, Lightfeather had broken her in on the heavy equipment used to level the ground for a drilling rig platform. For good measure, he taught her how to operate the same backhoe she was using now. Sherry was modest about her abilities and cherished Lightfeather for teaching her it was alright to be strong.

The metal detector indicated the box was four feet below the surface. Even though she hadn't used the backhoe in a year, she still remembered the basics. The earth was soft, and when Sherry reached her target, she played the backhoe levers with a lighter touch. She removed a few more loads of dirt before the hydraulics groaned when the bucket met resistance down in the hole.

The moment of truth was near, so she let the engine idle and the bucket hover above the center of the hole. She stepped down from the operator's seat and grabbed a heavy chain under the backhoe chair. She attached one end to the round metal eye on the underside of the bucket and dropped the rest of it into the hole. It landed on the top of the buried metal object with a satisfying clunk. Her heart raced, and her hands were damp while she shimmied down the chain.

The hole was well lit from the radiant sky above and Sherry saw the faint outline of the edge of the box beneath her feet. She anticipated some type of ring or hook in the center of the chest to facilitate lifting it out of the hole. When she dug in the dirt with the pointed tip of the chain's hook, she was rewarded for her efforts. Sherry pushed the dirt away to reveal a round eye, and promptly threaded several links through it.

She climbed out of the hole and jumped back into the cab. The idling engine vibrated the backhoe levers while she manipulated the bucket, tensing the chain and creating upward pressure.

The hydraulics groaned as the bucket tried to rise. For a moment, it was a tug of war with the box. With her hands firmly on the controls, her mind drifted for a moment while the sun warmed her face and cool, dry air flowed across her skin.

Sherry blinked as something shifted inside. The familiar aura that accompanied her hallucination signaled a transition. One that took her back twenty-five years to when she first experienced it.

Gone were the black and white hues that she had seen since she was twelve. Because now, on this Halloween day, the sky was incredibly bright and full of color for the first time. Young Sherry stood in an open field covered with hundreds of brilliant orange pumpkins, stacked one upon the other, rising over six feet high. At the bottom of the pile lay a straw scarecrow, dressed in shabby black pants and a chambray shirt. A large butcher knife glistening with blood slashed downward, again and again, eviscerating the scarecrow, leaving straw and shredded cloth to scatter in the fickle wind.

In her vision, a child gripped the knife handle, and she recognized his blood-stained weapon as a cheap Halloween toy. Costumed children dressed in vivid colors, danced around him and screeched in delight while he stabbed the straw man.

Watching over the mock assault was the grizzled giant from her childhood, named the Scarecrow Man. The gentle creature jumped up and down, clapping his hands, and urging the boy to assault his creation.

A gust of wind spawned dust devils, and the dry Texan wind whipped the children's costumes around their bodies, flapping against thin legs and arms.

Soon tiring of the mock assault, they ran across the street to the Halloween Carnival. With his audience gone, Scarecrow Man hung his head and mumbled, "It's Halloweenie." Jerking into motion, he shambled after the children and began walking down the street.

Young Sherry was in the middle of the pumpkins and a hand circled hers. She looked up at Mommy and saw her smile. "Love you, sweetie."

They walked across the street to a small grocery store and stopped at the counter to buy a pack of cigarettes. Sherry looked out the storefront window and a vague sense of urgency gripped her. The avenue was empty, and all the children were at the school carnival across the street. The pressure built into panic and she didn't understand what was happening, so she ran back to the counter. "Mommy?"

"Not now sweetie."

Sherry grabbed her mother's hand and jerked hard.

Mother swung around, irritation flashing in her eyes. "What's so important?"

The panic inside Sherry was unbearable. "The Scarecrow Man."

"What are you talking about?"

Sherry raised her hand and pointed to the street.

Mommy grabbed her cigarettes off the counter, looked up, and dismissed Sherry with a sharp look. "There's nothing out there."

The pressure inside Sherry was a deadly mixture of fear and anxiety. Mommy stared at her like she didn't understand. But Sherry had to do something. "Mommy, the man. Who'll save the Scarecrow Man?"

Mother whipped around and grabbed her daughter by the shoulders. "Stop it. I've had enough of your nonsense."

But the fear on Sherry's face caused her mother to glance back at the street. On the other side, the large grizzled giant called the Scarecrow Man shambled across the pavement without looking either way.

They both heard the powerful roar of a car, racing down the street, filling the store with its throaty echo. Sherry pointed at the Scarecrow Man. "Do something or he's gonna die."

Mommy's eyes opened wide and she screamed. The horrible screech of rubber on the pavement gave way to the crunch of metal meeting flesh and bone.

She stood frozen, hand to her mouth, "Somebody call an ambulance. *Now.*"

The clerk looked up and frantically dialed the phone while horrified shoppers rushed to the window.

Darkness twisted Mommy's face and she jerked Sherry around. In a fierce whisper, she hissed, "Don't ever do that again."

"But, Mommy, I...."

A crazy light shone through Mommy's eyes. "Sweet Jesus. What you did was evil." She gripped Sherry's face between her hands. "It's the devil inside you. Do you understand?"

Sherry's entire body shook as tears spilled over her cheeks. The crowd outside was growing larger and someone put a blanket over the Scarecrow Man.

Mommy stepped back, and Sherry saw the fear in her eyes. "Don't do that again."

In the space of a second, Sherry was back sitting in the backhoe with the slight rumble of the engine in her ears. Her mind was numb and on automatic. She was a million miles away and applied more pressure to the controls. Momentarily, the bucket surged upward and the box broke free.

For the first time she understood her hallucination. It was not a psychotic episode, it was the beginning of her psychic ability. Something that her twelve-year-old mind couldn't understand, and her mother, in her fear and fundamentalist religion, attributed to the devil.

Sherry couldn't save the Scarecrow Man.

She gently guided the small box upward and to the left of the open hole. After lowering the bucket, she leapt down from the seat.

Amid the turmoil of her revelation, something strange formed in her mind, squirming its way upward, just on the brink of consciousness. Sherry cleared her thoughts, took a deep breath, and waited for a piece to fall into place. Then she flashed to the psychic's house in Amarillo. In her first vision, she remembered Grandfather standing before her as a younger man, proudly erect and free of illness. His presence conveyed unconditional love, yet before his image faded, he imparted the cryptic words, '*Beneath the dead zone, Sherry. Find the cause and you will find your way.*'

Sherry lingered on his words just before she made a momentous leap to another message. When Grandfather lay dying at the hospice, her mind had entered the secret room. In this second revelation, Pablo, the black robed monk, stood in front of a crackling fire and said, *'When you were young, you were pure. You faced a path then. But on that fateful day, you lost your way.'*

On the edge of an epiphany, she struggled to understand the link between Pablo's and Grandfather's messages. Her mind refused to make the connection, so she shook off the uncertainty and focused on the mystery before her. The box on the ground was about two feet tall, four feet long, and two feet wide. There was a metal clasp on the side just waiting for her crowbar. She shoved the tapered end between the metal overlay and the side of the box. Sherry struggled with the heavy metal rod and really had to work it. Even though she didn't have the strength of a man, she was a determined woman. After a few minutes of sweating in the hot sun, she finally popped the clasp. She stood back, looked for an edge below the lid, and noticed a small crack along the top. Leveraging her weight behind it, Sherry struggled her way around the container until it came free.

Her heart thudded in her chest and she shoved the lid onto the ground. Adrenaline surged through her veins until she looked closer. The crystal was gone, the box nearly empty. Inside, was the small metal base that had been attached to the Atlantean crystal she and Cadence had seen in the cavern. Sherry removed the six-sided receptacle and revealed two weathered objects beneath it, an aged eagle's feather and a razor-sharp arrowhead.

She remembered Lightfeather's borrowed dish, the one sitting on the computer desk at the ranch house. Sherry realized that these two ancient relics were mementoes left by his Comanche ancestors. Her hands trembled, and she transferred the metal base to the cab of the backhoe and climbed inside.

Sherry retracted the backhoe's stabilizer legs and placed the bucket in its traveling position. The Cat engine revved and the wheels gripped the dirt, propelling the heavy equipment over the rough terrain. It was a twenty-minute ride back to the ranch house and her mind began to gnaw on the strange turn of events. Not finding the crystal was bitterly disappointing, so, she reflected on Grandfather's words.

'Beneath the dead zone, Sherry. Find the cause and you find your way.' Grand-

father didn't say, find the cause and you find the way. He said, *'Find the cause and you find your way.'*

She mulled this over and stared off into the distance.

The barren earth of the dead zone on Grandfather's land was caused by some residual force emanating from the buried metal base.

In a sense, what was below affected what was above.

Sherry took a sharp breath.

Understanding slowly unfolded in her mind and she grasped the parallel before her. When Grandfather said find the cause, he meant that when Sherry had turned her back on her psychic ability, she effected spiritual bareness.

When she had blocked her deeper intuitive self, it stunted her higher spiritual consciousness.

What was *below* affected what was *above*.

More of Pablo's words rushed over her and rang with internal truth. *'Your refusal to accept your true self poisoned your outlook. You think it has not affected you? From this vista, you chose unwisely. Your thoughts turned angry. Negative and self-destructive. Now your mind is confused, beset with trouble. But with each trial, God prepares an escape. You may still right the path and find your way.'*

Sherry's hands shook as the backhoe bounced across the rugged terrain. Just over the ridge, the ranch house came into view and she screamed in frustration, "Now that I've found my path, where does it lead? And where the hell is the crystal?"

THE EYE IN
THE SKY

AFTER THE FIASCO AT THE ranch yesterday, Morda disposed of his blue Mercury and purchased a generic white van. During the transaction, he intimated to the used car salesman that he would pay cash, a lot more cash than the vehicle was worth, if he didn't have to produce valid identification. When the salesman accepted his thick stack of hundred-dollar bills, it provided a refreshing boost to Morda's belief that humanity was basically corrupt.

He adjusted an air conditioning vent in the van and watched the traffic pass by the rest stop where he was parked. Favoring his broken left forearm, which was now in a cast, Morda opened his laptop and hit the power button. The computer was equipped with an air card, so he initiated a Google search for 'maps satellite' and waited for the screen to fill with its hits.

Something had bothered Morda ever since he'd left Sherry and Cadence in the cavern to die. After he'd snuck down the rope behind them, he'd watched the history of the ancient civilization burst across the wall. Morda was drawn to the scene depicting the awesome destructive power of the crystals. Yet, the physical characteristics of the land beneath the small box drew his attention, particularly the long narrow stretch of barren earth. Morda closed his eyes and vaguely remembered a similar spot when he'd initiated a real time satellite view of the ranch several days ago.

He brought up a mapping site with a click of his mouse and entered the coordinates for the ranch's rectangular shaped twenty-mile property. The long-distance satellite image showed the blurry beige of a semi-arid desert speckled with small patches of green. After a few more clicks, he zoomed in closer to capture the entire property on the screen.

From this bird's eye view, he didn't have the detail to locate the narrow patch of barren earth, so he finessed the image to focus on the outer edge of the property. Morda began to systematically search in small blocks from right to left, the picture so distinct he could see the scrub-like mesquite trees dotting the landscape, as well as the ruts in the dirt roads.

Morda studied each image carefully, confident that he would find the location. Yet, the minutes slipped by and his frustration mounted. He wiped his brow and looked up from the computer screen. On the other side of a nearby park bench was a family of quail, foraging in the prairie grass for food. Morda tapped his chin and wondered if he'd really seen the narrow landmark days ago. Had he just imagined it?

A few cars zipped by on the desolate highway and Morda flashed back to the cavern. After the ancient civilization's visual history had ended, Cadence traversed the cable over the small moated island and dropped down to join Sherry. His face twisted with discovery when he'd said, "Sherry, I know...." and then Morda had knocked him unconscious with the bat.

From his source within the FBI, Morda knew Cadence had tasked his remote viewers with finding the location of the crystal. Consequently, Cadence had gained employment at the ranch in order to find its exact location. Therefore, the crystal had to be on the sprawling property. Somewhere.

He refocused on the computer screen and clicked and dragged the mouse to reveal the last section of land. The final picture of the aerial view rolled across the screen and his tension mounted while he studied the real time satellite image. His heart missed a beat.

There it was.

A narrow stretch of bare earth about one mile from the ranch house. Yet something was odd about the image. Morda took a closer look and clenched his teeth. In the exact center of the barren soil was an excavated hole. To its left was a small open box.

He slammed the dash and screamed in rage. It couldn't be gone. Yet the proof was before him. Morda's source in the FBI had revealed that Sherry and Cadence had escaped from the cavern. That worthless slut had gotten to the crystal first. Morda checked his watch and estimated the time to have excavated the site and find the box. After a moment of calculation, it dawned on him that Sherry might still be in the area. With renewed purpose, he slowly moved the screen image toward the ranch house.

Bouncing across the rough terrain was a bright yellow backhoe. The same one that had unearthed the crystal.

Morda took a deep breath and started the van. He was parked a hundred yards from where the ranch road intersected the main highway and knew that he'd been fortunate this morning.

With a little more luck, Sherry would be leaving with the crystal shortly. Morda would be there to meet her when she hit the main road.

THE EARTH SHALL
SWALLOW HER
WHOLE

MOTHER SONJA SAT CROSS-LEGGED in the middle of her darkened living room in front of a flickering can of Sterno. Hungry flames licked the pan above it and tainted the room with smoke from her burnt offering.

Her plan was to entice Satan to do her bidding. Unfortunately, last night's chicken breast, aka 'the offering,' was just smoking up the house. It was also a bitch to keep Churchill from gobbling it up.

Slobber ran off his rubbery lips and the bulldog whimpered pitifully until the tiny psychic relented and tossed him what was left of the boneless breast. The sixty-five-pound dog snapped up the charred goodie in his powerful jaws, kicked his hind legs gleefully, and scampered out of the room.

"Good riddance," Mother Sonja squeaked as she contemplated her second spell to send that slut, Sherry, to the gates of hell. In preparation for this moment, she'd taken a cab ride to the local Spanish flea market, where she'd procured some Devil's Weed nutlets from a powerful female witch. The Bruja had instructed Mother Sonja to follow the simple instructions on her accompanying DVD for the arcane ritual to release the power of Satan. Mother Sonja gave the witch twenty dollars, shook her head as she left, and thought the dark world of spells and potions had gotten way too commercial.

Because of her limited vision, she separated the poisonous nutlets by touch and placed them in the small pan that had held the chicken breast offering.

The leftover grease popped and sizzled from the heat as she stirred the satanic concoction. Within moments a noxious vapor spread throughout the room.

The fumes stung her eyes and the psychic had to breathe through her mouth as she groped for a small bag of dirt to her left. With malice in her voice, she shrieked, "Oh, you sorry slut. You've got a surprise coming."

SHERRY PARKED THE BACKHOE ON the side of the workshop and killed the engine. In the ensuing silence, she contemplated the crystal's small, six-sided base as she picked it up. It was a half foot tall and weighed about three pounds. She remembered the scene in the New Mexican cavern, in which the hexagon base had a power input on its side, and held the bottom of the Atlantean crystal. The input receptacle allowed a power source to enter and transmit through the three foot long mineral. The final result would be a synergistic release of unimaginable energy.

The ancient technology that had unlocked the awesome power of this device was beyond her. Whoever obtained both base and crystal would yield unfathomable power. Sherry wrapped the receptacle in some rags from behind the backhoe seat and slipped it into her backpack. When she closed and locked the cab door, it was unclear why Cadence's remote viewing picked up the metal base and not the crystal itself. Perhaps the strong remnant of its energy signature, the same one that had caused the barren earth above the box, was to blame. Maybe the remote viewing target wasn't properly defined.

Her plan was to drive the motorcycle into Amarillo and pay a visit to the county Sheriff's downtown office. She knew there was a leak at the FBI and didn't want to fall into that trap if she could help it. Sherry was still unsure if that was the right thing to do.

It was a quick walk into the workshop where Sherry removed the motorcycle cover on Daddy's BMW and fired it up. A small puff of smoke shot from the exhaust pipes and the opposing force of the twin cylinders vibrated the handlebars beneath her hands. She backed the motorcycle out of the shop and onto the drive, ready to take her shortcut over the septic tank. While she listened to the thrum of her idling engine, she felt the tickle of a forgotten memory, something Lightfeather had said a few days ago about the septic tank. But, for the life of her, she couldn't remember what it was.

MOTHER SONJA COULDN'T RECALL WHAT the Spanish *Bruja's* DVD said about preparing the Devil's Weed. Should it have been ground or heated? She was pretty sure it should have been ground and not heated, because two blurry cans of Sterno were weaving before her eyes. There was this odd sensation in the pit of her stomach, like she was going to puke her guts out any moment.

She fought the nausea and reached for the bag of dirt. Her gnarled fingers latched onto the sack as she shoved one hand inside to scoop out a mound of soil. The two cans of Sterno had now multiplied into three, and she fought hard to keep from passing out. Her hand weaved back and forth before she dumped the dirt into the pan above the flame. The psychic closed her stinging eyes and took several shallow breaths. Under normal circumstances, the best she could see were vague forms. But, when she reopened her eyes, she was stunned with unrivalled clarity.

In slow motion, the flame from the Sterno licked the edge of the pan, then abruptly shot up three feet and morphed into a hideous face. Mother Sonja had done a lot of acid in the sixties, but she'd never experienced anything like this. The grotesque face wavered before her eyes and its mouth opened wide. From that black hole, the stench of rot and decay gusted forth, churning her already uneasy stomach.

The creature's eyes were pits of intense evil and its split tongue flicked outward testing the air.

Malevolence permeated her already compromised soul and she knew she was in the presence of true evil. Even though she was at the fork of a spiritual crossroad, her years of hatred and deceit made the choice almost easy. She willingly crossed the line.

"You have summoned the one who is." The mask of evil acknowledged her unspoken commitment with words of whispered silk.

Mother Sonja couldn't look away from its horrible beauty. She tried to speak, but only choked out, "I...."

The mouth grimaced hideously, and a hiss spewed from its throat. "I know what lies in your heart. Pain and revenge is the task you set before me."

She managed to nod yes.

"As you wish it, so shall it be."

The flames of the demonic head parted to reveal the small mound of earth that Mother Sonja had dropped in the pan.

In her state of enhanced visual acuity, she opened her clenched fist and saw, for the first time, the intrinsic detail of Sherry's heart-shaped charm.

She extended her arm to the edge of the parted flame and hesitated. A soft evil laugh filled the room as the psychic pushed through the opening and dropped the charm in the center of the coned earth. When she pulled her hand back, the demonic flames rebirthed the face.

Hellish flames gushed from its open mouth and shot upward in a stream of Satanic fire, reaching toward the ceiling, before turning downward to pummel Sherry's charm.

A horrible stench filled the room as the cone of soil collapsed with a steaming hiss. Just before passing out, Mother Sonja thought she heard, "And the earth shall swallow her whole."

SHERRY HESITATED BEFORE SHE SHIFTED the BMW into gear to enjoy a stolen moment of natural wonder. A soft autumn breeze rustled the native grass and caressed the heart of this vast prairie. While the blue sky above complimented the majestic golds and browns of the prairie below, she felt her spirit open to the gentle beauty of this vast wilderness.

Whenever she needed a fresh perspective on life's problems, she immersed herself in God's beauty and embraced His gift called Texas. This moment of quiet reflection added motion to her desire to bypass the FBI with her discovery of the crystal's base.

She cinched her motorcycle helmet, punched the BMW into gear, and glided across the soft mud of the parking lot. The tires slipped a bit until she reached the shortcut leading across the septic tank.

She was close to the luxuriant grass that was nurtured by the human waste below when something clicked inside. Sherry finally remembered what Lightfeather had said the other day. "Stay away from the septic tank. The ground's a little soft."

She hit the brakes and slid to a halt. The ground didn't look any different from the last time she had ridden over it, but Sherry didn't want to take any chances, so she angled the BMW around the septic tank and hit the gas. The motorcycle's shock absorbers cushioned the rough terrain while she sped toward the road. When she reached out to adjust the rearview mirror, Sherry glimpsed at the reflection and gasped. The ferocious power of falling earth shot vapor and raw sewage thirty feet into the air. And now there was a gaping hole where the septic tank used to be.

What the hell? That ground looked more than a little soft.

YOU CAN RUN, BUT YOU CAN'T HIDE

SHERRY GLIDED TO A STOP where the ranch road intersected the main highway, looking both ways before turning right. With precision born of practice, she slammed through the gears and ripped up the road until she hit the speed limit. Her decision to approach the county Sheriff with the crystal's base was finally sitting well as she shifted in the motorcycle seat. Sherry would be in their office within thirty minutes and put an end to this drama.

Cadence had been on her mind all morning. It broke her heart to know he would be a vegetable for the rest of his life. Sherry prayed now that Morda's ass had been kicked, the bitch had left town.

Cool air flowed across her face. The road was clear, the midmorning sun pleasant. But, the rev of an engine from behind caused her heart to stutter. She glanced in the mirror and saw a white van that was way too close. With a flip of her hand, she waved for the driver to pass. The engine roared when it pulled ahead, but the van slowed, paralleling her in the passing lane. When the passenger's window rolled down, Sherry shot the driver an irritated look. Looking closer, she noticed the ugly snout of a gun pointed at her head.

It was the devil's handmaiden, Morda.

The bitch gestured with the gun for Sherry to pull over, but Hell would freeze over before that happened. Sherry knew what the slut was capable of. Falling into Morda's hands again wasn't going to happen.

Sherry locked the back brake down and the van shot ahead before Morda realized what had happened. Dropping a few gears into third, she hit the nitrous switch and twisted the throttle hard. The effect was instantaneous. The speedometer shot from forty to eighty-five in a matter of seconds and Sherry popped it into fourth and rocketed past Morda before the psychopath could react.

There was no stopping now. Sherry would put as much distance between them as possible, because she knew what Daddy's motorcycle was capable of.

Sherry glanced in the mirror and saw the van accelerating, trying to keep up. The vehicle probably had a large engine, but vans like that weren't made for high-speed pursuit.

Ratcheting the gears up to fifth, the brute force of her nitrous driven engine accelerated so ferociously, the flesh on her cheeks creased. She ate the road up until the van started to recede. The speedometer hit one hundred and thirty miles per hour and kept on climbing.

Sherry was in the middle part of the Road to Hell and her thoughts turned to her father. An unexpected sense of gratitude bubbled within her because it was his motorcycle that allowed her to escape. She looked at the speedometer and it was pegged higher than she had reached before. Fortunately, there were ten miles of straight highway ahead and she knew Morda couldn't keep up. Just to be sure, she checked the mirror and saw the white van a mile back.

The crystal's base was in her backpack and the road ahead was clear. A smile spread across her face just before she heard a gut-wrenching sound. The speed of her BMW began to decline from 140 to 120 and then settled on 100 mph. She had failed to fill the nitrous tank after her last ride.

Sherry was faced with a devastating problem. She couldn't outrun Morda, and on this desolate road, there was no place to hide. Just miles of open prairie.

The white van was eating up Sherry's lead and she was desperate for a strategy. The closest town was the small college community of Canyon, Texas. If she got there first, she could ditch her bike, find a phone, and call the police.

Considering her cell phone was back at the ranch, this wasn't much of a plan. But it was all she had.

SURPRISE, SURPRISE

SHERRY ROARED DOWN THE MAIN street of the sleepy college town of Canyon, Texas. With a quick look in her mirror, she saw that Morda's van was three blocks behind and closing in fast. The whine of her pursuer's engine split the air behind her as Sherry did the unpredictable. She locked her rear brake down, went into a controlled skid, and shot left down a narrow alley. Slamming through the gears, she rocketed past trash dumpsters and the back doors of restaurants and small businesses. In twenty feet, she reached the main thoroughfare and blasted left onto the avenue. A small apartment complex was on her right and had a short walkway that entered an enclosed courtyard. Sherry jumped the curb, bottomed her shock absorbers out, and blasted down the sidewalk, into the safety of the enclosure.

She killed the engine, dropped the bike on the grass, and rolled to safety behind a small bush. Moments later, Morda's van screamed by.

Sherry got to her feet, ran to an apartment, slammed her knuckles on the door, and was greeted by silence. Another door, another knock, more silence. The complex was as dead as her hope, until Sherry realized why. A poster on the wall heralded the college's annual Rodeo Roundup for this morning and the student population was at the West Texas Coliseum.

With immediate phone access cut off, Sherry looked across the avenue at the university's museum. The door was open, so she moved to the edge of the courtyard and looked both ways. The road was clear, foot traffic nonexistent, so she cinched up her backpack and raced across the street. At the top step of the museum, brakes screeched, and she glanced at the road behind her. Morda had doubled back. When the slut opened the van door, she jumped out and smirked. Thirty yards separated them, and Sherry ran to the museum counter for help, only to see a sign that read, *Back in twenty minutes.* Behind the wooden desk, were three entrances that offered three places to hide. Sherry sprinted into the Historic High Plains exhibition, running down a path leading to an 1800's pioneer dugout. The walkway twisted past a Plains buffalo hunter skinning bison hide and ended at a High Plains Indian Tipi.

Morda's feet slapped against the floor, stopping at the desk. She hesitated in front of the three entryways. The Indian diorama Sherry stood in front of had a small rope to keep visitors away, so she climbed over and entered the buffalo hide Tipi. Desperate for a weapon, she saw a pair of medicine man shakers—three feet long wooden sticks with pebble laden turtle shells on one end—propped inside the structure. Sherry closed the flap of the Tipi and grabbed her unlikely weapons. The sign behind the shakers caught her eye.

Comanche Borrowed Items, Circa 1850.

As she gripped the painted shafts, it was apparent they were not wood, but six-sided crystals. Sherry reread the sign and looked closer at the two objects. Her heart clutched in her chest. How friggin' unreal. She remembered the eagle feather and arrowhead tucked under the crystal receptacle she had just unearthed.

Had she really found the crystals of Atlantis?

One appeared to have an etching on its side, about halfway up, but was covered with reddish dye. She reached into her pocket for a fingernail file and scraped the coloring off to reveal a human eye centered inside a pyramid. While more dye flaked off, Sherry's hand encircled part of the bare shaft. Her scalp tingled, and the crystal began to pulse an ambient yellow, casting its light inside the Tipi. A golden hue filled the Indian lodging as a three-dimensional scene unfolded before her.

The image revisited Amelius, the spiritual and political leader of Northern Atlantis as he struggled with his emotions in the center of the Priest's Chamber. It showed his granddaughter, Aiyala, the seer, as she connected with the Prophet's crystal.

Aiyala, who had an uncanny resemblance to Sherry, lifted her head and spread her arms to embrace the light. She inhaled deeply of the golden essence within the room, causing it to ripple and pulse while it slowly revolved around her.

Centered within her luminous aura, she spoke firmly, decisively. Her voice resonated with strength. *"Show the path, oh God of One, so that we may free the enslaved."*

A three-dimensional figure of Atlantis materialized above the crystal in the amber mist. The Divine image confirmed the treachery of the south's leader.

Massive shafts of energy pulsed from their war machines and impacted the cities of the north. Towering fire consumed the dead and those too maimed to flee. Since the full power of their crystals was used, tectonic plates beneath the island nation were impacted, causing earthquakes that destroyed the homes of the north and the south.

Amelius would not survive, nor the population of Atlantis.

Aiyala, alone, would live, escaping with the Prophet's Crystal and one offensive weapon.

The image faded and the ambient light around Sherry subsided. She gripped the Prophet's Crystal in her right hand and was psychically aware of three things. She was the reincarnation of the young seer, Aiyala. Lightfeather was the reincarnation of Amelius. And Mother Sonja, the reincarnation of the southern Atlantis' leader.

Sherry had finally found the missing crystals and knew she needed to leave. Now. But when Morda parted the flap and pointed her 9mm at her, that thought died an uneasy death.

Morda nodded at the crystals. "Let's go for a ride, bitch."

MORDA PRESSED THE GUN AGAINST Sherry's back as they walked past the unmanned museum counter and down the empty street to the white van. The psychopath slammed the side door open and got up in Sherry's space.

Morda's face held a mixture of animosity and triumph, which was why Sherry didn't see the rapid sweep of the gun until it crashed into her jaw.

Sherry collapsed in a heap inside the van and felt the sting of a needle in her hip. An image of Cadence in a vegetative state came to mind and she prayed that wouldn't be her fate too.

Just before Sherry passed out, Morda blew her a kiss.

WHAT DID YOU PUT IN
MY COCKTAIL?

THE ODDEST SENSATION FLOWED THROUGH Sherry's body. Her forehead bounced against warm flesh as if being carried on someone's shoulder. Her mental acuity was buried in a vat of blackstrap molasses. The scary part was, she didn't know why.

Questions began forming themselves in her fuzzy mind. Why would someone be carrying me? She imagined that she was Queen of the Nile and a giggle squiggled out of her throat. She pondered the word squiggled. Was it really a word?

Her head stopped bouncing when her royal bearer halted. The metallic clang of a door handle being pulled signaled a change. Sherry's slave lifted her up and dropped her in the interior of a cool metallic chamber, where her skull hit the floor with a thump. She giggled again. This was way cool.

Sherry's head spun when she looked around. She thought Cleopatra would've killed for a ride like this. The interior was painted dark green and there was a round barrel next to her marked with black stenciled letters. *DANGER, HIGHLY FLAMMABLE.* For some reason, that was insanely funny. Sitting on top of the barrel was a box with small red numbers that flashed *12:00…12:00…12:00.*

Her royal slave jumped inside and slammed the door. "Take us up."

Was being graced with a female slave politically incorrect?

It might not be in vogue, but if the shoe fit, she'd wear it.

There was a whine from somewhere and the royal ride began to shake. In a few moments, the rear end lifted and a loud *WHUP-WHUP-WHUP,* echoed inside.

Sherry looked out the window. The ground slowly disappeared and she had a strange feeling in the pit of her stomach. Something was amiss in the kingdom, but for the life of her, she couldn't put a finger on it.

MOTHER SONJA MOANED WHEN A HOT, wet tongue slid up her neck and across her jaw. Sensation fluttered in areas she'd thought were gone forever as she reached up to caress her lover's head. She ran her fingers through his short bristly hair and felt another wet caress higher up on her cheek. She sighed and opened her eyes just as Churchill's massive tongue slid across her lips leaving a thick paste of drool in its wake.

The psychic wobbled upright and scrubbed her mouth with the back of her hand. She screamed, "Jesus H. Christ," and watched Churchill waddle away. She looked around and wrinkled her nose from the God-awful stench in the living room. It took her a moment to piece together what happened before she passed out. Her head throbbed like a bitch, and her vision was a fuzzy blur. The can of Sterno was extinguished and she finally remembered her summoning spell to set Lucifer upon Sherry.

Mother Sonja closed her eyes and tapped into her psychic ability to see if Sherry was still alive. After a moment, it came, and the answer infuriated her. The slut was still breathing.

If you got a job to do, you gotta get people you can depend on. The psychic paused in thought, waiting for her path of action to crystallize. She rose to her feet and hobbled to the living room closet. She threw the door wide open, digging through years of accumulated trash until she found the small gray urn.

She grabbed Grandmother's ashes, or 'Cremains' as the funeral director called them. Satan had fucked up, but the departed spirit of her blood kin and mentor, would not. Mother Sonja shrieked in glee as the final solution unfolded.

DID THE ANCIENT EGYPTIANS HAVE backpacks? Sherry pondered that for a moment when her slave slipped a hand inside one, removed two awesome crystals, and gently placed one in a small metal base that lay on the floor of the royal ride. The slave reached over, snared Sherry's wrist, and jerked her to a sitting position.

That insolence was totally out of place. If Sherry weren't in such a good mood, she would have bitch slapped her.

The slave leaned closer. "Do you know who I am?"

Sherry studied the woman's thin, angular face. Noted the long blond hair that cascaded past her shoulders. Her skin was flawless alabaster and she had some killer nails. All Sherry could offer was, "Uh, you're my slave?"

"Wrong. The name Morda ring a bell?"

A warning light went off in the back of Sherry's mind, but she couldn't connect the dots. She shook her head. "Everything's kinda fuzzy right now."

Morda bitch slapped her. Pain ratcheted inside Sherry's brain and she vaguely remembered something slamming into her head earlier. She gingerly touched her jaw and felt dried blood on top of swollen skin.

We're not in Kansas anymore, Toto.

And Morda was the wicked bitch of the east.

Morda tapped her forefinger against her flawless cheek. "You said your mind's a little fuzzy. Like to know why?"

Right now, Sherry had a mondo case of cotton mouth and couldn't answer. She bobbled her head yes.

"Roughly an hour ago, I chased you down and retrieved the two crystals you found in the Canyon museum. Fortunately, I got the upper hand."

Morda leaned closer and smirked. "I pistol whipped you and gave you an injection before you passed out. It was a twilight cocktail with a bit of scopolamine and morphine. All designed to keep you docile until the big finale."

Sherry's attention wavered, and she started to lie back down, but Morda jerked her wrist hard. In the process, Sherry's charm bracelet broke and she watched it drop next to the end of the metal-based crystal.

Morda grinned and Sherry wanted to knock that smile off her face.

"Now that I have your attention, Sherry, I'm sure you'd like to know what I have planned." Morda's eyes sparkled with mirth. "You see, Lightfeather and Leitha are back at the ranch house and you're going to drop in on them. Literally. You, a fifty-five-gallon drum of methanol, and a lump of plastic explosive. Like they say in Texas, Sherry, yee-haw. And guess what? You'll have the best seat at a real Texas barbecue."

Alarm bells were ringing like crazy in Sherry's mind. Lightfeather and Leitha were in danger, Morda, the royal slave, had a few screws loose. And someone was going to fire up the barbecue.

MOTHER SONJA SNIPPED THE END off of a six-foot extension cord with her rose shears and pulled the two rubber-sheathed wires apart. She bit down on the insulation of one strand and pulled until she exposed three inches of bare wire.

She stripped the other strand and shoved the two copper wires deep in the ash on opposite sides of the urn so they weren't touching. Pleased with the positioning, she got up to plug the extension cord into the wall socket.

Churchill snorted from the kitchen and she braced herself for the hardest part of the final solution. Her hands trembled when she placed the sharpened tip of her rose shears against her left palm. She closed her eyes and jerked the edge downward, tearing through her parchment-like skin, leaving a three-inch diagonal wound.

The gash began to seep and gave way to an ooze that quickly ripened to a steady flow. The psychic winced while she held her palm above the urn, sacrificing her life force to raise the malevolent spirit of her Romani grandmother. Rivulets of blood poured down her palm and she smelled its coppery tang as it puddled in the center of the urn.

The blood mixed with the ash, turning it black while it seeped into the heart of the cremains. Within a few minutes, it spread outward from the center, creating an ungodly, dark sludge.

When the blood completed an electrical conduit between the two exposed wires, a dangerous hum filled the room. Tiny veins of electricity emerged and jerked across the top of the cremains, convulsing on spidery legs.

The potent combination of Mother's hatred and high voltage appeared to be working. Now all she needed was her grandmother's spirit to kick in.

Churchill poked his head into the living room just as the veins of electricity reached over the edge of the urn. The probing tendrils strobed outward, across the carpet, leaving singe marks wherever they touched. Mother Sonja realized there was a conscious force behind the display, because none of the electrical wisps came near her.

Grandmother's spirit was on the edge of crossing an invisible barrier, ready to explode in a latent rush. The moment had finally come.

She reached over to the burnt offering pan and dug through the dirt for Sherry's heart shaped charm. Her gnarled fingers sifted through the charred soil and connected with the silver trinket. She clasped it tightly and pressed her fist against her chest. With a shrill howl, she summoned the dark force of her mentor. When she threw the charm into the center of the gray urn, she violated the barrier that held the spirit in check.

Mother Sonja croaked, "Free the thunderbolts and fry that sorry bitch."

A loud explosion shook the room and Churchill raced back to the kitchen. The few lights that were on, burst, and flames shot out of the wall socket where the extension cord was plugged in. The fire quickly receded as a thick, acrid smoke billowed from the connection.

She looked back at the urn and felt her Grandmother's influence. The tiny tendrils of electricity that crackled with lethal intent moments before now grew into jagged veins of malevolent energy. Energy that ripped across the walls, ceiling, and floor.

A brilliant magnesium glare violated the dark interior of the living room while the stench of something old and decayed assaulted her nostrils. A swirling cloud of gas rose from the center of the urn and billowed outward until it dimmed the electrical maelstrom to a dull glare.

An image slowly formed within the ominous cloud. Mother Sonja recognized the likeness of her grandmother, but the face was hideously twisted and distorted. Horrible creases lined the forehead and the eyes were pools of tortured insanity. Grandmother had dark rotten stubs for teeth and her hair hung in matted clumps around her scalp.

When the entity opened her mouth, the screech of a thousand lost souls abraded Mother's ears.

Grandmother's gaseous face rose to the ceiling and gradually grew smaller, until her features collapsed into a white-hot sphere. The scores of crackling veins that had emerged from the urn still jerked around the room with manic energy. But now, the small sphere acted like a beacon that attracted and absorbed the random lightning. When each vein connected with the orb, a harsh explosion split the air.

The basketball-sized vessel pulsed like a beating heart and grew brighter with each electrical charge it absorbed. Mother Sonja's hair stood on end from the intense static electricity and the hum she'd heard earlier ripened to a high-pitched roar.

The floating orb continued to devour the chaotic shafts of energy until none remained. Smoke from a hundred scorched spots inside the room produced a suffocating cloud. The psychic's attention was riveted on the pulsing vessel of her grandmother's spirit.

The bottom of the sphere seemed to dissolve, while a thin shaft of molten energy flowed downward into the urn holding Sherry's charm.

Mother choked on the smoke and clapped her hands. Between coughs, she shrieked, "Kick her ass, Granny."

THE EFFECT OF THE TWILIGHT drug faded and desperation gripped Sherry. It began to register that she was in a helicopter with Morda. They were on the way to incinerate Lightfeather and Leitha. There was also some strange shit going on with her charm bracelet. Just a second ago, a pulse of energy haloed around it, and now it was pumping an incandescent charge into the metal base holding the crystal.

Morda was on the other side of Sherry leaning against the wall with her 9mm. From where Morda stood, the bitch couldn't see the energy being channeled from Sherry's bracelet into the crystal. That was good for now, but it was later that Sherry worried about. The power of the crystal was devastating, and she didn't want to be around when it cut loose.

At this point, her choices were insanely terminal. She could try to overpower Morda, who had a gun and wouldn't hesitate to shoot. Then there was the pilot, who looked like a pit bull on steroids. Sherry was in desperate need of divine intervention because this was a no-win situation.

While Morda gazed out the window at the city below, Sherry frantically looked for a weapon. Her eyes roamed the inside of the barren cargo area, and she scanned the length of Morda's body. Something in the shadows caught Sherry's attention and gave her a rush of hope.

Oh my God. A parachute.

Over a year ago, she completed the training to take her first skydive, but washed out before she made the jump. So, Sherry knew how to put the chute on, but didn't know what to do after that.

She snuck a peek at the crystal on the opposite side of the methanol drum. The shaft was beginning to glow from a rising charge of energy and, fortunately, Morda still couldn't see it.

All Sherry had to do was wait.

In the space of a heartbeat, opportunity beaconed when an intense energy beam shot out of the opposite end of the crystal. It hit the metal divider separating the cargo area from the pilot, producing a small wisp of flame. The concentrated energy punched through the steel and ripped into the pilot's torso.

The man screamed in mortal agony and slumped over the controls. The helicopter lurched forward and the fifty-five-gallon drum of methanol slid directly toward Morda.

It slammed against her with a quarter ton of dead weight and pinned her in the corner. Morda dropped her gun and shock distorted her face. She tried to push the barrel away, but she couldn't budge it with only one good arm.

Sherry wobbled across the lurching floor and tried to snatch the parachute by Morda's feet. The bitch was like a cornered animal, lashing out to pummel Sherry's face and neck, landing a few jarring blows on her body. Sherry finally grabbed the chute and scuttled toward the door. The helicopter lurched violently, and it was all she could do to step into the leg harness and keep her balance. She pulled the bottom rigging up past her thighs and shrugged into the top webbing. It was like putting on a backpack. Finally, she fastened the latch against her chest and secured the parachute.

Sherry reached for the sliding door handle. The helicopter was in a sickening fall and the crystal slammed against the dividing wall. A deadly stream of destructive energy sliced through everything it touched. Only a few inches separated the beam from the flammable drum of methanol.

She glanced at the dead pilot and checked on Morda, who was still pinned in the corner and doing her best to get loose.

Sherry threw the door open, grabbed the Prophet's Crystal, and put a death grip on the hand rail while the wind blasted through the cargo area. The force almost knocked her off her feet. Nausea ripped through her stomach. Terminal impact was imminent, and panic seized her soul. She gaped at the approaching ground and remembered why she had washed out of skydiving a year ago.

She was still terrified of the free fall.

UP, UP, AND AWAY

CAPTAIN ZOTT—AKA HARVEY BERNSTEIN—took a toke on his home-grown Maui and leaned out the window of the Amarillo Astoria Hotel. Twelve stories below was a supersized stuntman's air bag, fully inflated and ready to commemorate the loss of his super powers and personal demise.

Unfortunately for Harvey, a plot twist for the crime-fighting Captain Zott was on the drafting board—just in time to resurrect the hero for next week's installment. But today, his adoring fans would see their hero plunge to his death.

Twenty years ago, during a marijuana marathon with his stoner buddies, Harvey took their dare to audition for the children's TV part. And, in a cruel act of fate, he'd gotten the job. That first script was geared for the grade school Malt-O-Meal crowd and had soon nose-dived in Harvey's estimation to capture the post-Gerber gang.

Harvey's self-esteem had plummeted steadily over the years while his popularity rocketed. It was bad enough that he had to dress up in an insipid crusader's suit, but he also had a throng of adoring fans. At weekly appearances around town, the sticky-fingered, snot-nosed mutants would mob him while he gave rides on Captain Zott's Spaceship. Every time they squealed in unison, *"Captain Zott! Captain Zott! Come on, show us what you got,"* Harvey turned beet red and cringed from embarrassment.

In his estimation, all children were badly-behaved midgets who needed a prolonged caning.

Harvey was in a pensive mood and moved back inside the open window. Taking a final drag on his joint, a seed popped inside the burning stub that he pinched between his thumb and forefinger. He held the smoke in and flipped the roach out the window. Watching it plummet downward, Harvey thought it was an ironic symbol to his twenty years of creative stagnation and lost dreams.

He'd begged the producers early on in his career to update the show's format, give him some freedom to expand his character. But their only concern was the advertising revenue the program generated and local product endorsements.

Harvey had come to a fork in the road. Should he continue to milk the cash cow of Captain Zott or follow his dreams? In his heart, he knew it was time to move on to greener pastures.

The sad truth was, other than an active imagination, he didn't have any employable skills and had been out of the job market for two decades. Harvey crossed his arms and stared glumly at the sky.

The camera crew was set up on two locations to follow Captain Zott's final exit. One was on the roof of an adjacent building and the other on the ground by the supersized air bag.

A voice buzzed in his earpiece, *"Camera team ready. On my mark, one minute and counting."*

Harvey looked up at the sky and heard the steady *whup-whup* of helicopter blades. Then, for just a moment, there was an eerie silence. He shaded his eyes and looked high above to see a Vietnam-era chopper begin to drop.

A little voice inside Harvey spoke and for the first time in twenty years, he listened. In a rush of creative insight, he grabbed the hand radio and screamed at the camera crew, "There's a helicopter crash coming in at twelve o'clock. I want both cameras on it NOW."

SHERRY STOOD NEAR THE OPEN door of the cargo area and her heart beat so fast, light flashed behind her eyes. Her legs buckled, and her insides wiggled like a bowl full of gummy worms.

It was down to the bare bones now. There was one fact she couldn't escape—she would die if she stayed in the helicopter. The only alternative was to jump and take a chance on the parachute.

She told herself it was a no brainer and shuffled to the edge of the platform. Her whole body trembled. Unfortunately, Sherry's momentum put her at the point of no return and she embraced total emptiness. The harsh wind ripped at her clothes and howled in her ears as she plunged toward the ground.

The gale force wind brought tears to her eyes and blurred her vision. Sherry was virtually blind and couldn't see the rip cord that opened her chute. She frantically patted across her upper torso and reached above in case it was blown out of place by the wind.

After five attempts she still couldn't find the damn thing. Panic crippled her mind. She was falling at terminal velocity and impact was just moments away.

TRAPPED IN THE CORNER OF the cargo area, Morda heaved against the drum that pinned her to the wall. Crippling pain ripped up her broken forearm and kept her from using that limb. She jerked and shoved with her good arm but couldn't move it.

Unless something happened soon, she would die. Facing her own mortality, there were no images of loved ones flashing before her eyes, but the discordant sounds of Janette's *Ave Maria* filled her mind.

The blind German violinist was the only one remotely close to Morda, and Janette's Godless rendition of the holy song always brought Morda comfort.

Morda's eyes rolled upward and she took a deep breath. The harsh strains of music had a narcotic effect upon her as she reveled in the spiritual desecration Janette had created.

Smiling in anticipation, Morda refocused on the cargo area. Janette now stood across from her, playing like she always had. Her savage bow ravaged the strings, giving life to a voice of spiritual violation. The violinist moved with consummate passion, giving her deepest emotion to the performance, somehow touching and filling the void within Morda.

Janette's starched white shirt emphasized her hardened nipples and her long blonde hair was gone. Blood flowed from a wound in her temple.

She slowly lowered the violin to her side and stared at Morda with dead sightless eyes. Her lips barely moved as she said, "I'll always be there for you."

A psychotic howl rippled from Morda's throat, rising above the roar of the wind. In a moment of blood frenzy, Morda murdered Janette two years ago then sheared the long blonde hair off of her head.

The very hair that Morda now wore.

Even though it was pleasurable to see Janette, more important things needed tending. Morda wasn't ready to die. Arching her back against the corner of the cargo area, she leveraged her pelvis against the barrel, put both hands on the rim of the drum and heaved. Red-hot pain ripped up her broken arm, but she kept pushing until the container moved a few inches.

It was just enough.

Morda scrambled over the drum and jumped to the floor. In the back of her mind, she remembered the prophetic power of the crystal skull, foretelling her plunge from the helicopter. In an effort to cheat death, Morda had brought a parachute for backup. That was all for nothing.

Rushing to the edge of the open cargo door, Morda scanned below. Sherry was a small spot still plunging downward. She clenched her fists in impotent rage.

Until she focused on the ground below.

In the courtyard of a tall hotel was a supersized airbag used by stuntmen to break high elevation falls.

Elation surged within her, but then quickly passed. Morda was too high to survive landing on the airbag and needed to be closer. She also required something to slow her fall. Morda frantically ransacked the cargo area until she found a large medical supply box. Ripping through the contents with manic intensity, Morda uncovered a thick, wool blanket.

A desperate plan formed while she rushed back to the door. Gripping two corners of the blanket in either hand, Morda envisioned a canopy that would form a crude air brake and slow her fall.

There were two parts to the equation. On one hand, the helicopter was steadily angling toward the airbag. The second part of the equation reeked of uncertainty. Even if she jumped from the helicopter at the last moment, would the airbag break her fall?

Morda knew that the truly insane lacked the ability to reason. What she was going to do fell in the realm of madness. But Morda was functionally insane and possessed an ability to create her own outcomes. So, with the final strains of *Ave Maria* in her mind, Morda cursed the God who created her and waited for the chopper to get closer to the bag below.

Even if she survived the fall, where the hell was the helicopter going to crash? When Morda looked at the drum of methanol and plastic explosives beside her, she began to sweat.

WHAT GOES UP MUST COME DOWN

HARVEY BERNSTEIN KNEW THAT A pivotal moment was occurring, and he wasn't going to miss his golden opportunity. A person was in terminal freefall and the spiraling helicopter wasn't far behind. Harvey mashed the transmit button on his radio and spittle flew from his mouth when he screamed, "Camera one, stay with the falling body. Camera two, cover the chopper."

Both operators responded with a ten-four, their voices charged with excitement. History was in the making for Captain Zott and Harvey's fertile imagination conjured up a resurrection for his toilet bowl career. The helicopter crash would form the platform for a new story line and allow him to breathe life into his career nemesis, Captain Zott.

Harvey quickly scribbled his thoughts on a piece of paper. Government conspiracy, mysterious helicopter crash, and a plummeting body. Captain Zott unravels the clues. With his imagination in overdrive, Harvey buried his guilt as the chopper's falling occupant came closer to certain death.

SHERRY GROPED AROUND HER BODY, trying to find the ripcord. Her mind was totally scrambled, and she screamed in raw fear. The hard concrete loomed below.

A glimmer of hope stirred within. Down below, there was a large airbag in a nearby courtyard. In parachute training, they said you could glide and move about by positioning your body. She leaned forward in an effort to sail closer. Because of the restrictive harness, she was unable to fully stretch out.

Sherry tried to posture herself like she was diving into a pool. but the wind buffeted her body when she leaned forward, launching her into a series of flips and turns. Totally disoriented, she couldn't stop her motion.

HARVEY LEANED OUT THE TWELFTH-STORY window when he saw the first jumper begin tumbling out of control. Much to his surprise, a second person leaped from the plunging helicopter. Amazingly, a small canopy spread above the second jumper, billowing outward like a tiny parachute.

He didn't know how much stranger things could get.

SHERRY FINALLY THREW HER ARMS out and used her upper chest to catch the wind. She jerked her head back, which stopped her uncontrolled spinning. The rushing wind roared in her ears and she gulped air so fast, she hyperventilated. Her heart beat out of control, ready to explode, as she was moments from a horrible death.

There was nothing she could do.

FROM THE HOTEL WINDOW, HARVEY looked up and put his hands to his cheeks. The first jumper was moments from impact. When he heard a small pop, he couldn't believe his eyes.

A LOUD BANG STARTLED SHERRY and sound rippled above her, like a sheet snapping in the wind. In rapid increments, the chute deployed itself and jerked her upward while the parachute captured the wind. The deadly fall had become a controlled descent.

Sherry grabbed the parachute risers above her shoulders and her body went limp. She didn't have a clue what had just happened but swore she would never skydive again.

HARVEY IMMEDIATELY KNEW WHAT HAD happened. He recognized the altimeter release mechanism that deployed the chute at a preset height.

From his vantage point, Harvey watched a woman gently drift toward the street in front of the hotel. Keying the radio again, he commanded, "Camera one, capture the parachute landing, then cut to the helicopter. Camera two, transition to the second jumper."

Within moments, the female landed safely on the ground, and Harvey's Jewish guilt over her fate eased greatly. But the drama wasn't over. He keyed in on the second jumper's strategy, a landing on the stuntman's airbag. There was a dangerous catch. The falling helicopter was on a collision course with the building in front of the airbag.

The second jumper was dead on target with the stunt bag, but was coming in fast—way too fast to survive a landing.

The jumper hit the middle of the airbag and a ferocious whoosh of air shot out as it cushioned the fall. A second later, the helicopter hit the top of the office building across the courtyard. Fire ballooned into the sky, and Harvey flinched from the intense heat.

A second explosion ripped through the guts of the chopper and shattered nearby windows. The horrific force catapulted the twisted wreckage upward, over the edge of the building.

With his mouth wide, Harvey watched the wreckage plummet to the courtyard below, dropping twelve stories, landing squarely in the middle of the airbag.

Intense flames incinerated the fabric. In the distance, Harvey heard the wail of multiple sirens.

There was no way the second jumper survived.

BYE–BYE, BABY

TWO WEEKS LATER, SHERRY BORROWED Lightfeather's truck to run some errands in town. On this bright, cheerful morning, she navigated the Interstate traffic on the way to the Georgia Street Starbucks. Slowing the vehicle for the coming exit, she engaged the turn indicator just when her cell phone chirped. It was an unfamiliar number, but she answered anyway. "Hello?"

"Is this Sherry Whittington?"

"Yes, who's calling?"

"I'm Jane Boston with the Highland Nursing Home. I've been asked by Cadence McShane's aide to relay a message. It's important that you get here quickly."

The breath caught in Sherry's throat. A dozen scenarios ran through her head, none of them good. She navigated the exit in a daze. "Has anything happened to him?"

A brief silence ensued before Jane coughed. *"I'm sorry, all I know is that Jill passed along this message. She didn't elaborate further."* The caller took a quick breath. *"I don't know any more."*

Sherry hit the end button and threw the cell by her purse. The nursing home was close to the Starbucks and she floored the accelerator. The engine roared and she careened down the exit ramp, turning left onto Georgia Street. The four-lane road was lightly traveled this morning, which suited her fine. She was doing fifty-five in a thirty mph zone, when the traffic light turned red. Her hands were sweating on the steering wheel and she was hell bent for leather. Sherry looked both ways, punched it up to sixty-five and ran the bitch. The next two lights were green, and then she blasted past the Starbucks, squealing onto the two-lane road leading to the nursing home.

It's important that you get here quickly.

Sherry raced into a visitor's parking spot, slammed the truck in park, and jumped outside. A mad sprint up the sidewalk put her at the door. An uncomfortable pain throbbed in her chest when she entered the facility. The hallway was empty, and Sherry ran the last few feet to Cadence's room. She burst inside, and he was on the hospital bed with his hands folded on his stomach. His IV drip was still in place, the catheter bag half full. A profound sense of relief rushed through her when she saw the gentle rise and fall of his chest.

Thank God. He was still alive.

She let her pulse settle before picking up a stack of Amarillo newspapers on the easy chair. Sitting down beside him, she began to worry about the reason for the urgent call. The murmur of voices outside and the scuff of rubber-soled shoes on linoleum filtered their way into the room. A squeaky wheel on a trolley rose in pitch and faded away. Somehow, this conveyed a sense of normalcy, a feeling that the world was still a safe place. Sherry brushed her hair into place and glanced at the newspapers on her lap. A week-old headline screamed out, **PET SAVES MASTER FROM FIERY DEATH**. She scanned the picture of a burnt-out house and did a double take when she read the first few lines.

Mother Sonja, a local psychic, narrowly escaped a fiery death yesterday afternoon. Fire inspectors determined the cause of the blaze as an electrical short in the living room's wall socket. The psychic, who was unconscious on the couch was roused by the frenzied barking of her pet bulldog, Churchill.

The corners of Sherry's lips lifted in a slight smile and she felt an odd sense of satisfaction. God works in mysterious ways, doesn't He? She dropped the papers on the floor and looked up to see Jill enter the room.

Her shawl was drawn around her neck, her face pinched when she came to Cadence's bedside. Jill put her hand on Sherry's arm.

"I wanted to be the first to tell you...."

Sherry's stomach twisted in knots.

"But, I'll show you instead."

Jill moved to his bedside and gently squeezed his arm. She said, "Cadence, you've got a visitor."

Sherry moved next to Jill and stared down at Cadence's face. Moments passed and he still didn't respond. Sherry glanced at Jill. "Are you sure he's...."

"Alright?" Cadence replied.

His eyes fluttered open and a faint grin enhanced his roughish charm.

Sherry's heart skipped a beat and tears welled up. She pressed her hand to her mouth. "I thought that you were—that this—was permanent."

Jill punched a button and raised the head of Cadence's bed. "From what you told us about your encounter with Morda," Jill explained, "she administered one shot in the cavern while Cadence was unconscious. The drug brought on a time released, semi-vegetative state that lasted over two weeks."

Jill pursed her lips. "Toxicology tests couldn't identify the substance. We were totally stumped. All we could do was care for him and make sure he was comfortable. Then yesterday, he opened his eyes and gradually regained consciousness. It was a matter of deduction about the time release."

Jill gave her a sweet smile. "I waited until he was fully recovered before I called you."

Sherry looked down at Cadence and wiped her tears away. "Even though Morda had the upper hand in the cavern, she still lied about the duration of the drug's effect."

"She had to have total control over us," Cadence explained, "By painting the bleakest picture she could, she also took away our hope." Cadence's face softened when he looked up at Sherry. "By all rights, you and I should be dead, but because of your brave actions, we survived."

There was a moment of silence until Jill cleared her throat. "I'm sure the two of you need some private time, so I'll come back later."

The soft swish of stockings and the squeak of the door closing marked her departure. Cadence's eyes shone with gratitude and his emotion warmed Sherry's heart.

"How much do you remember after you blacked out in the plane?"

His face darkened with anger. "Morda didn't lie when she said I'd be aware of everything. It was a living nightmare, particularly when we landed and I couldn't help you with Lightfeather."

Sherry squeezed Cadence's hand and brushed his hair back. "How much longer will you be here?"

"They had me walking earlier. That's why I was asleep when you arrived. With a little luck, I'll be gone in a week."

Cadence moved his hand and looked away.

She stepped back and crossed her arms. "So this investigation's closed then?"

"Pretty much. Since the crystal was destroyed, the threat to national security is a moot point."

"What about the people behind Morda?"

"We had some leads, but there's not enough evidence to charge them."

Sherry summoned her courage and asked the next question, "Where will you go from here?"

Cadence's voice was unemotional, "Probably somewhere in the Southwest. Another investigation."

A sharp pain shot behind Sherry's eyes. "I guess that means I won't see you again."

His eyes were flat as he looked away. "Yeah, well, I'm going to be really busy."

Sherry's world was beginning to crash around her, until she saw the grin on Cadence's face.

"I'm going to be busy for the foreseeable future in Amarillo, Texas. So, sweetheart, I hope you don't mind having me around."

She punched him on the arm for scaring her, then took both his hands in hers. This scenario worked on so many levels for her.

DID YOU SAY PABLO?

SHERRY PULLED INTO THE CEMETERY where her grandfather was buried, listening to a Rolling Stone's song come to an end. She opened the truck door and walked along the path leading to the cemetery's small chapel. When she stepped inside, the darkened interior was aglow from candles set upon tables flanking the altar. Five wooden pews were on either side of a carpeted pathway leading to the front of the chapel. Sherry noticed a rail-thin, elderly woman with a high-tech walker. Elegantly dressed, the lady stood a little over five feet tall and had short, spiked black hair. She held a pomegranate energy drink in her hand, and in the mesh web of her walker, she had five or six empties inside it.

The black-haired woman drained the bottle and dotted her lips with a small handkerchief.

"Did you know," she asked, holding the bottle up, "If I'd invested in this stuff rather than mortgage-backed securities, I'd be rich now." She snapped her fingers and a light went on in her eyes. "Can't forget why I'm here, now can I?" She added in a conspiratorial tone. "It's a little something you'll be needing soon."

She dug inside one pocket of her black velour pant suit and removed a business card. With a flourish, she handed it to Sherry.

On the front was the name *Johnnie*, in big bold letters. But when Sherry turned it over there was nothing on the back. No number or address, just Johnnie. Rather strange. But the psychic tingle Sherry felt inside told her there was more here than met the eye.

The candles near the altar fluttered from some unseen force and Sherry was drawn to this likeably odd woman. "Excuse me, but who are you?"

"I'm an intuitive counselor. But my day job is a TV chef on the Southern Food Network channel."

There was not a glimmer of deceit on her face.

"Well, Johnnie, are you here for a 9-1-1 intervention on my pot roast, or are you helping with something more metaphysical?"

Johnnie just smiled and took a pack of non-filtered Camels from her pocket. She tapped one out, flicked her lighter and took a deep, satisfying drag. When she exhaled, the smoke spread throughout the small chapel, taking on a golden glow from the candles.

The pixie-like woman put her hand on Sherry's arm and winked. "In life, you don't always get what you want." A look of profound wisdom darkened her eyes, "But sometimes, you'll get lucky and get what you need."

Her statement got Sherry's attention. "Just exactly what do I need?"

"A good cook should always share her secrets. When the time is right, you'll see me again."

Sherry was about to press the point, when pain spiked across Johnnie's face. She blanched as her hand fluttered to a small box suspended on a chain around her neck. She twisted a knob and within moments, her cheeks flushed with color.

A sheepish grin brightened Johnnie's face. "Got a bad element in the oven, and had a pacemaker installed a couple of years ago. Seems like energy drinks bring on erratic heart beats. But when you really like something, sometimes you gotta suck it up. Or fix it. So, I had an electronics whiz create a gizmo that amps my heart rate up and overrides the arrhythmia." She patted the box and grinned wickedly. "And man, what a rush."

Just before Sherry was about to ask more questions, tires crunched on the gravel outside. The opening from "La Cucaracha" blared from the vehicle's musical horn.

Without missing a beat, Johnnie whipped her walker around and scurried across the chapel floor. She stood by the exit, and asked, "You remember Pablo, don't you? He told me to give you his regards."

Just before the chapel door closed, Sherry heard the driver outside yelling in Spanish. Johnnie gave him a gangsta hand sign and shrieked in return, *"Hola, Pablo, que pasa?"*

Sherry was frozen to the spot. It *can't* be him. She sprinted to the door and heard tires spin on the gravel. Rushing outside, she saw the tail end of a Lincoln Navigator rocket down the road.

Totally bizarre.

The only Pablo Sherry knew existed in her vision. This had to be a freak coincidence. Didn't it? It took her a moment to shake off the apprehension, yet there was a tingle in her spine when she walked to Grandfather's grave.

Dappled sunlight passed through the protective canopy of the oaks above on the way to his grave. A gentle prairie breeze stroked the native buffalo grass and billowy clouds formed magnificent columns that rose ever upward. Their pristine presence stirred her soul and the deep blue sky humbled her with God's spirit. She was subtly reminded of the fragility of human life, but ever so grateful for its gifts.

Sherry sniffled and looked upon the freshly turned earth. Grandfather was such an important part of her life and she missed him deeply. She scuffed her shoe against the soil. Did he know she was here? Sherry whispered to his spirit, "Grandfather, if I could speak in the tongue of angels, would you hear me?"

The comforting sound of prairie birds called across the grassland and the wind was soft upon her face. What tribute could she give to a man whose strength and legacy was unconditional love?

Anything she could do would fall short, but precious words formed beyond conscious thought. Sherry opened herself to the presence within. Tears formed in her eyes and rolled down her cheeks. "Grandfather you're bound upon the gossamer wings of moonbeam and sunlight. And, even though we're but a breath away from the face of God, I can hear you whisper through the veil. This is not goodbye, it is merely a pause 'til we meet again."

Sherry gazed off into the sky, lost in thought. The spirituality of her tribute filled her with the precious coin of comfort. Yet, as with all things in life, the beauty of his tribute passed, and she was left with the fleeting grains of its spiritual essence.

She took a deep breath and mentally changed gears. It was finally time to reflect on some issues from the past week. Sherry was not proud of the fact that she had psychically probed Cadence when he was catatonic. When she was holding his hand in the plane with Bob, she mentally asked him who was behind Morda and who wanted the crystal. The answer stunned her because it wasn't a person. It was an organization. The John Adams's church. A longtime recipient of Grandfather's financial support.

Cadence would never know that she had lifted this classified information from his subconscious mind. Sherry preferred to keep it that way. She had also reached an understanding with her psychic ability. The fact that it could be used for good far outweighed the fear her parents had planted within her mind. Anything could be used to do evil. It was the intent of the user that determined the outcome.

Another detail remained. After Sherry's dramatic exit from the helicopter, she saw Morda plummeting toward the stuntman's airbag. After the psycho-path hit the cushion, Sherry's attention was focused on the helicopter when it crashed into the building across the courtyard. There was a horrific explosion and the wreckage was blown off the building. It fell into the middle of the air-bag—exactly where Morda was last seen.

In the cleanup process, two things were sought—the crystal and Morda's body. Because of the force of the explosion, only minute pieces of the offensive weapon were found. Yet there was no trace of Morda, bones or otherwise. The authorities speculated that the intense heat from the methanol might have in-cinerated her remains, but it had to get really hot to consume human bones.

There was another tidbit no one else knew. Sherry had not given the Proph-et's Crystal to the FBI, because her newfound psychic ability hinted at a broad-er mission. There was a spiritual obligation she had to fulfill, going back twelve thousand years. Until that debt was settled, it would stay in her possession.

She knew Morda was still out there. As long as Sherry had Aiyala's crystal, she would be looking over her shoulder.

There would be more to come.

MICHAEL DAVID graduated from West Texas A&M in 1988 with honors, earning a BBA in Finance. For the next two years, he worked as an assistant examiner for the F.D.I.C. during the banking crisis of the late 80's. By that time, though, Michael had decided to heed the call of becoming a writer and quit his job in 1990. He found a job in Amarillo, Texas working with people with disabilities and began writing.

He is the author of five novels and two screenplays, and is currently under contract with publisher Oghma Creative Media for three manuscripts.

Michael is now retired, and resides with his wife in Amarillo, Texas where he is an active member of the writing community.

michaeldavidauthor.com

www.ingramcontent.com/pod-product-compliance
Lightning Source LLC
Chambersburg PA
CBHW032006240626
47153CB00003B/1147